"I was terrified he wasn't gonna make it."

Neal carefully tucked the tiny kitten back beside his mother. "It still may be touch-and-go." He caught Tessa's eye over his shoulder. "Do you know when the vet's office opens? I'd call for an appointment right away."

Tessa tried to remember what the answering machine message had said. "Seven thirty, I think?"

Neal checked his watch and straightened up. "He's gotten his airway clear. He should be okay until then."

"You're a hero. I should write something up about you in the paper for this." *Tourist Pulls Off Early Morning Kitten Rescue.* Pretty adorable as headlines go.

"I'd rather you didn't." There was an edge to his words. Then again, she had yanked him out of bed on his vacation. Still, being a reporter gave her a nose for a story, and Tessa could tell there was something behind his immediate and curt refusal. People normally loved to be in the paper, and there was always a deep reason why someone wanted to stay out of view. What was his?

Allie Pleiter, an award-winning author and RITA® Award finalist, writes both fiction and nonfiction. Her passion for knitting shows up in many of her books and all over her life. Entirely too fond of French macarons and lemon meringue pie, Allie spends her days writing books and avoiding housework. Allie grew up in Connecticut, holds a BS in speech from Northwestern University and lives near Chicago, Illinois.

Visit the Author Profile page
at LoveInspired.com for more titles.

Secrets of Their Past

Allie Pleiter

LOVE INSPIRED

INSPIRATIONAL ROMANCE

LOVE INSPIRED®
INSPIRATIONAL ROMANCE

ISBN-13: 978-1-335-40970-6

Secrets of Their Past

This edition published by arrangement with Harlequin Books S.A.

For questions and comments about the quality of this book, please contact us at CustomerService@Harlequin.com.

Love Inspired
22 Adelaide St. West, 41st Floor
Toronto, Ontario M5H 4E3, Canada
www.LoveInspired.com

Printed in U.S.A.

Chapter One

*Q*uiet.

Tessa Kennedy had forgotten how good quiet sounded. She looked out over her backyard to the glory of a Colorado mountain sunrise, watching the steam rise serenely from her coffee cup.

A quiet Monday morning like this hadn't happened in ages. Not with the chaos of a teenage son. Greg was a one-man tornado of temper and hormones, and they'd locked horns so many times in the past three weeks, she was worn thin from the strain. Even on the drive to the airport yesterday afternoon to spend most of July with his dad, Greg had stomped on her every last nerve.

She loved Greg. She tried to be grateful for the young man he was becoming— most days. But being the single mother of a teenage son was a long, exhausting up-hill climb. *I'd be lying, Lord,* she thought as the sun's rays washed the back deck in a brilliant glow, *if I said I wasn't grateful for the break from it all. Just for a little while.*

Three whole weeks of peace and quiet felt like the grandest of luxuries. Her fingers found the edge of the notebook that had lain untouched for far too long. *I can finally do this.* The thought invigorated her as much as the brisk mountain air. *I can finally write more than small-town news.*

She had no dreams of *The History of Wander Canyon* being a bestseller. Tessa wasn't even sure it had to see publication. It just had to be done, and done by her. She wasn't a woman given to bucket lists, but if she had one, this would top hers. She loved the idea of documenting the history of Wander Canyon and the families who called it home. After all, it was her history. She was a third generation Wander Canyon resident, and that story needed to be explored as much as the greater story of the whole town.

Silence and writing. Tessa closed her eyes and reveled in the idea. What could be more blissful than that?

Mew.

Her eyes opened at the strange sound.

Mew. Mew. A tiny chorus of *mew*s, in fact.

Someone had moved into the vacation rental guesthouse next door yesterday, but she'd caught a glimpse of him. A veterinarian on vacation, the rental host, Valerie, had told her.

Mew. Mew.

Tessa tried to peer through the boards to the space under her porch. It sounded like a litter of kittens.

There's a litter of kittens living under my porch? It seemed impossible for her not to have noticed that before, but the way Greg shouted and pounded and played music all day, perhaps it wasn't so hard to believe.

Not giving a thought to the fact that she was in pink polka-dot fuzzy socks, Tessa rose and padded down the steps.

Kneeling on the grass in purple-plaid fleece pants, Tessa leaned under the porch to spy a cat and a litter of kittens.

The cat she recognized. It was a fat black-and-white neighborhood stray, one Tessa had named Doug—for no other reason than the name had popped into her mind when she'd seen the animal. The cat had seemed too independent and wild to be anything like a Whiskers or a Fluffy, so somehow the simplicity of Doug had fit. She'd fed Doug every once in a while, but the cat never came close or showed signs of wanting to be friendly.

"You and every other eligible Wander Canyon male," Tessa had quipped a week ago when Doug had gobbled down his food, given Tessa a blank look and then wandered back into the bushes. A single working mom didn't have much time for dating, but it would have been nice to try to schedule a few dates. Tessa didn't know whether to be pleased or annoyed that Doug had chosen to have her litter under the back porch.

Tessa peered a bit closer. "Well, I think we all know now you're not a Doug." She tried to think of female names starting with *D*. Tessa liked country music, so she peered a bit closer and asked, "How does Dolly sound?"

Dolly gave Tessa a wary *I don't care what you name me, just keep your distance from my babies* look. "I'll take that as a yes. Congratulations, Dolly. Fine family you've got there. What can I do to help? Why don't I go see if Greg's left anything in the house that you might eat and I'll set it out for you."

She was turning to go when a small

gasping sound met her ears. The heart-breaking, tiny choke stood out among the other little mews. One of the little guys sounded as if he were struggling for breath. Was there anything sadder than a kitten in trouble?

"Hang on, Dolly. I'll get some help on the way for your little one."

Tessa sprang into action, scrambling back to the deck table for her cell phone. Not owning a pet of her own, she had to look up the number of Wander Canyon's only vet, Dr. Davidson.

No answer. After all, it was 6:28 a.m. Wander wasn't big enough to merit a twenty-four-hour veterinary service for anything other than large animals. And even that was two towns over. A gasping kitten sounded both too urgent for the distance and not urgent enough for the practice.

It might have been a wiser choice to get into some decent street clothes before pounding on the door of the house next door, but lives were at stake. She could apologize later, after Dolly's tiny kitten was out of danger.

"Um...hello?" the man said with an irritated yawn, running a hand through his dark hair. It ought to be illegal that a man could look like that straight off the pillow. Tessa needed at least twenty minutes—and two cups of coffee—to look human. That meant she probably was a rather shocking sight, but emergencies were emergencies. "Can I help you?"

"I'm your neighbor. I live right here." She tilted her head back toward the house, alarmed to find a tuft of grass fall out of her hair from her trek under the porch.

"Hello," he said again, clearly trying to make sense of why Wander Canyon residents roused their new neighbors at unreasonable hours.

"I think I have a veterinary emergency under my deck, and Valerie mentioned you." Suddenly she was embarrassed to know such facts about the man, but Valerie had given her a quick heads-up on the man who would be her neighbor for the next month. "Could you...um...? Do you think you could come take a look?"

Her new neighbor ran a hand down his face and across his dark stubble. "Wander Canyon doesn't have a veterinary practice?"

Was she really hearing desperate little mews behind her, or just imagining them? "Wander Canyon doesn't have a vet *who's answering his phone* at the moment, no."

She gave him her best pleading smile. "Please?"

He hesitated, much to her dismay, but after a few seconds, he held up one hand. "Give me a minute."

"I'll wait right here," she called as he walked back into his house.

Tessa leaned down and tried to peer through the latticework on this side of the porch. She couldn't see where Dolly and her kittens were. Straining her ears, she heard the little mews—and the pathetic tiny cough. It was now 6:34 a.m. Tessa tried to tell herself one kitten was no big deal, not really an emergency. *Hang in there, little guy*, she pleaded, half to the kitten and half to God. It would be *wrong, wrong, wrong* to start the first day of her long-awaited summer break with the demise of a kitten.

Two achingly long minutes later, the man opened the door in a yellow T-shirt, a pair of jeans and sneakers still unlaced. He shifted a black canvas bag—the vet version of the classic doctor's bag, she assumed—to one hand as he pulled the door shut behind him.

He turned to her. "Show me where."

"Over here," Tessa called as she began running to the far side of her porch. Had the tiny sounds stopped? "I'm not sure one's gonna make it," she added, feeling even more foolish for how her voice choked up on the words.

"I'm Tessa, by the way," she said, remembering her manners as she bent down by the opening where Dolly was. "There's this one little guy… It sounds like he can't breathe."

"Neal," the man replied as he crouched next to her.

Tessa knelt. Maybe he was going to ask her to pray for the kittens.

He looked back at her, laughed and said, "Um…my name is Neal."

Tessa felt her face heat up. "Oh. Right. Sorry. My name is Tessa."

"So you said," Neal reminded her as he peered under the deck. They both watched Dolly react with a protective hiss.

"This isn't your cat?"

"No. I feed her every once in a while. Actually, up until this morning, I thought it was a him." Suddenly the whole situation felt overblown and silly. "I'm sorry. It's probably not okay to bother you like this."

He managed a reluctant smile. "Kittens in crisis. You had to do something, right?"

Neal peered farther into the space, assessing. "Hello there, mama," he said in soft, soothing tones. He unzipped the bag and pulled out a set of latex gloves.

"Dolly," she offered, suddenly feeling even more foolish.

"You called a cat you thought was a male 'Dolly'?" he said as he pulled on the gloves with a practiced ease.

"Well, no. I swapped out Doug for Dolly just now." It sounded absurd as she said it, and Tessa felt her cheeks heat up even more.

"Dolly it is, then. Congratulations on all those little babies, Dolly."

"It's the gray one," she urged from behind him. "The smallest."

"Yep," he replied, still facing the litter. "I see him. He's got some trouble going on."

"Can you do anything?" Tessa found herself actually rocking back and forth on her knees.

Neal got down lower, folding himself in order to get farther under the deck. "That depends on the mom." His voice became very low and musical. "Mind if I take a look at your little guy?"

"Come on, Dolly. Let the nice doctor give you a hand." *Stop babbling and let the guy do his job*, Tessa lectured herself. This wasn't exactly the best way to meet the man who was going to share your driveway for the next month.

"Okay, Dolly," Neal said, "I'm going to move nice and slow. No reason to be afraid."

Tessa peered over his shoulder as Neal reached in beside the mother cat. She hissed at first, but eventually let his hand move through the rest of the kittens to reach the small gray one. She realized the wheezing had stopped. Her heart broke at the still form curled in Neal's hand as he pulled the kitten into the light. *No. Come on, Lord. Pull this one out of the fire, won't You?* she prayed as Neal began tenderly examining the kitten.

"Hmm." He murmured, "Okay then,"

as he lifted paws, peered at ears and eyes. Finally, he reached back into the bag and pulled out a stethoscope that seemed as big as the tiny kitten's head, fixing the earpieces in place before slipping the metal disc against the white, furry belly. He closed his eyes while he listened.

Tessa couldn't really say what he did next, only that whatever he did resulted in a sudden flurry of movement and sound from the kitten. She fought the urge to applaud.

"Blocked airway," Neal said as he sat back on his haunches, pulling the stethoscope from his ears. "But his heart doesn't sound too good. He's okay for now..."

"For now?" Tessa said. "But..."

"You'll need to get him checked out by your local vet. He'll probably need some ongoing care. The little guy's got issues."

Tessa gave a sour laugh. "Don't we all." After a moment, she gushed, "I don't know how to thank you. I was terrified he wasn't gonna make it."

Neal carefully tucked the tiny kitten back beside its mother. "It still may be touch and go." He caught her eye over his shoulder. "Do you know when the vet's office opens? I'd call for an appointment right away."

Tessa tried to remember what the answering machine message had said. "Seven thirty, I think?"

Neal checked his watch and straightened. "He's gotten his airway clear. He should be okay until then with his mother and the rest of the litter."

"You're a hero. I should write something up about you in the paper for this." *Newcomer Pulls Off Early Morning Kitten Rescue.* The sheer cute factor alone would be worth how annoyed it would make Dr. Davidson.

"I'd rather you didn't." There was an edge to his words. Then again, she had yanked him out of bed on his vacation. Still, being a reporter gave her a nose for a story, and Tessa could tell there was something behind his immediate and curt refusal. People normally loved to be in the paper, and there was always a deep reason why someone wanted to stay out of view. What was his?

Tessa peppered him with questions about kittens and respiratory issues, and whether or not feral cats were safe.

After patiently enduring the barrage, Neal finally looked at his watch and said, "So, do you have time this morning to get them all to the vet?"

"Of course," she agreed. "Wait… They *all* go to the vet?"

"I'd advise it. I've still got a box at my place—do you have a blanket we can use?"

Tessa hadn't even considered the tricky bit of getting Dolly and all her kittens into a box. Dolly didn't appear too eager to leave her spot under the porch. All seven of the kittens, plus Dolly? That sounded dicey at best. Still, Neal had just said "we," hadn't he?

"Get your box. I'll get one of Greg's old shirts or something, and I'll meet you back here," she replied. "I'm sure I'll need your help to get them into the box and then we can go visit Dr. Davidson."

"I can help you get them into the box and then *you* can take them to the vet." If Neal didn't speak the words *because I'm on vacation* out loud, his eyes did the talking for him.

"Of course," Tessa agreed. She wasn't even going to bother to call and make an appointment. Next stop was going to be Dr. Davidson, if she had to camp out in the parking lot until he unlocked the office's front door. "Thanks, Dr…." she said, cueing him to fill in his last name.

"Rodgers. Neal Rodgers. And we can skip the *doctor* bit for now."

"But then you'd be Mr. Rodgers, wouldn't you?"

No smile crossed the man's face.

"Get it?" Again, no response. "Yes, well,

probably not the first time you've heard that."

Neal's weary expression hinted that Tessa might not have gotten off on the best foot with her new temporary neighbor.

When Tessa returned with two of Greg's old sweatshirts, Neal piled them into a cozy nest inside the box he'd brought. With gentle tones and slow movements, Neal expertly coaxed Dolly and her babies into the box with minimal hissing and no sign of scratches. Still, a tiny wave of mewling protests filled the air as he shut the lid.

I wouldn't have even thought to shut the lid, Tessa thought, grateful once again for his help. "You're a godsend," she said sincerely.

He shrugged as if he didn't agree. "I'm sure your vet will know what to do."

"Of course. Thanks. Again."

"You're welcome." With that, he headed off across the backyard to his own side door.

Tessa hurried upstairs, tossed on some

clothes and tucked the box into the back seat of her car.

All the while, she tried not to think about how she may have irritated this "Mr. Rodgers" on his first day in her neighborhood.

Chapter Two

Neal stared out his kitchen window and tried to make sense of the last hour.

He should be annoyed that Tessa banged on his door and demanded he play vet rescue so early in the morning. After all, he was supposed to be on vacation. He'd done his research to make sure Wander Canyon already had a practicing vet. His time here wasn't professional; it was personal. Exceedingly personal.

So how had he managed to end up doing exactly what he didn't want to do? How had she convinced him to step in?

Her eyes, that was how. Tessa had bright

blue eyes under all that bedraggled hair. Eyes that had been filled with worry. Over animals that weren't even hers. He'd be lying if he said he didn't find her level of drama a bit amusing, but not in a bad way. He tried to think of the word for her over-the-top urgency. *Endearing* came to mind, but that sounded too gooey. After all, he saw that sort of panic all the time. Pet owners frequently got emotional over their animals. It touched his heart—or, at least, it used to.

His vet tech had chided him more than once in recent weeks for growing a short fuse. The fact that his compassion had gone AWOL was part of the reason he was here.

Neal had been shorter with Tessa than he'd needed to be. She seemed nice— sweet, almost, in a down-to-earth, small-town way. He hadn't been sleeping well, and the early morning knock hadn't found him at his best. *She's going to be your neighbor for the next month*, he chided silently. He quoted his own words to himself. *Kittens in crisis. You had to do something, right?*

He got up from the table and pulled a Pop-Tarts package from one of the four different boxes in his cabinet. Neal liked to think he didn't have many vices, but the breakfast pastry was chief among them. *Mom would give me one of her looks*, he thought as he bit into the first one without toasting it. Toasting was for amateurs— true Pop-Tarts lovers didn't need to warm them up. *I'm a grown man. I don't need a mother to tell me what I can or can't eat for breakfast.*

Yes, well, a mother was one of the reasons he was here in Wander Canyon trying to find his compassion again. Was this tiny Colorado town the place to get it back? Neal wasn't sure. He caught his pathetic reflection in the kitchen window glass and lectured himself. *If you can't manage to be nice to someone facing a kitten in crisis, you really do need this trip.*

Neal replayed their conversation as he polished off the two Pop-Tarts. Tessa had wanted him to tell her the kitten would be just fine. He couldn't do that. Neal made it a policy never to lie to people. Every vet knew it was bad policy to make promises you couldn't keep.

No matter the sweet concern in Tessa's eyes, he couldn't promise her a happy ending. Not every kitten made it, no matter how adorable. Sometimes life just dealt you a short hand from the get-go, and all the wishing in the world didn't change that.

Neal shaved and indulged in a second package of sugary pastries, annoyed at how often he peered out his window. Waiting for her car to return? To see if she came home happy or crushed? The sudden urge to know irritated him, and assured him that maybe his compassion wasn't gone for good, just temporarily lost.

Her last name was at the top of a lot of things he didn't know about his neighbor.

She was nervy; he knew that. Knocking on his door at that hour, insisting he lend a hand?

And she was nosy. She seemed to know a lot about him. She knew he was a vet on vacation and that he'd be renting the house for a month. Was it just her, or were small towns always like that about newcomers?

The best thing would be to keep his distance. He knew himself well enough to recognize he needed solitude to think things through. Time among the magnitude of the mountains and the vast clear sky would lend him the perspective he needed to sort things out. He needed to be left alone.

And that was a problem, because Tessa didn't strike him as the leave-you-alone type. He should have taken that other cabin farther out of town. Or maybe he should have never given in to the impulse to come to Wander Canyon in the first place. This should have been the last stop on his journey to understand the wounds of his childhood, not the first.

Well, you're here now. All you can do is try to make the best of it.

When Tessa's car finally pulled up, Neal headed out his side door. Even as he told himself not to get involved, he met her as she gingerly lifted the box of mewling cats out of her back seat.

"I'm gonna keep 'em," she declared without any further explanation.

Eight cats? He couldn't help raising a dubious eyebrow at her pronouncement.

"Well, not all of them," she added in answer to his expression. "I'm not gonna be some crazy cat lady. Just the little guy."

Without any explanation, Neal knew she was referring to the sickly one. A lost-causer—he should have seen that one coming. Years in veterinary practice had given him a pretty sharp instinct for people given to hopeless causes and taking in strays.

She smiled at him with those wide,

overly friendly eyes. Neal suddenly wondered if he wasn't giving off some lost-cause stray vibe without realizing it. After all, those words could indeed classify the reason he was here. And Tessa certainly wasn't letting up on her attentions to him.

What was the safest response? The truth was that the kitten might not survive. It was easy to see she'd be crushed if that happened. He ought to offer her some warning. Some sage advice on the dangers of becoming too invested in an animal of questionable health.

Instead, he said nothing. Neal just couldn't bring himself to go there. Not with her. *You're on vacation*, he argued with himself. *This animal isn't your responsibility. You're not her vet, and she's not your friend.*

Tessa, of course, picked up on his silence. "I mean, he's going to be okay, right? Doc D says it's too soon to tell, but I've got a feeling about the little guy." Her eyes did that thing to him again he was trying hard to ignore.

Like any good vet, Neal had a sensible speech he gave to distraught pet owners at times like these. One he hoped she'd heard from this Doc D, if the man was any decent kind of a veterinarian. A balanced, caring yet cautious set of words that never promised a certain outcome.

He bit back the speech, just shrugging instead. *Coward.*

A very small meow came from the box as she started carrying it up her back porch steps. Halfway up, Neal realized he was following her. "He's a fighter," she declared as she set the box down and opened it to reveal Dolly and her litter. "Greg will love him."

She'd mentioned a Greg as the source of the worn shirts currently nestled around Dolly and her kittens. "Does your husband know he just adopted eight cats?" If there was one surefire way to tank a new pet's chances, it was not making it a family decision. He'd seen it a hundred times.

She bristled at his question. "Greg is my

son," she replied in sharp tones as all the warmth left her eyes. "And as for my ex-husband, he has absolutely no say in the matter."

Son? He hadn't seen a child anywhere around the house, but he had only been here a day and a half. Hadn't seen a man, either, for that matter. What business was that of his, anyway?

"Greg is at his dad's in Utah for three weeks." She squared her shoulders in—dare he say it?—endearing defiance. "So this is my decision."

"Okay then." What else was he supposed to say? She'd made up her mind. Besides, he was in no position at the moment to call anybody else on a bad plan.

Tessa put her hand in the box to pet one of the kittens, and Neal was pleased her gesture wasn't met with a hiss from Dolly. Not every stray consented to become a house pet. "I was wondering what to do for my other project while Greg was gone," she said as she gazed at the cats. "I guess I have my answer."

"Your other project?"

"I like to have at least two going at any time. You know, so you can still get progress on one when the other hits a snag." She rearranged the shirt and Neal waited for Dolly to object. She didn't. "I've been multitasking since before they called it that."

To Neal's surprise, Tessa reached into the box and lifted the tiny little cat he knew she'd chosen to adopt. Animals, for the most part, had good instincts about people, but Neal tried not to read too much into the fact that Dolly seemed to welcome her family's new champion. "Say hello to Charlie."

"Dolly and Charlie?" Somehow he knew there was a wacky reasoning behind the names.

"Country singers." She sat on the porch's top step and pointed to the kitten in her hand. "You've met Dolly and Charlie."

She then pointed to each of the box's feline occupants in turn. "That's Blake, Johnny, Reba, Kenny, Patsy and Loretta."

Neal felt he had to say it again. "But you're not going to keep all of them." In his experience, naming eight cats was just the first step on the slippery slope to owning eight cats.

"Doc says I need to keep them all together for another eight weeks, but I can keep Charlie for good when he's weaned. And Dolly, if she stays. But she might not. She's an independent woman who might like her freedom."

People projected human qualities on animals all the time. Some—many—animals were better than people. It was why he preferred them to humans most times.

She had this all planned out. Was he going to be able to stay uninvolved while Tessa nurtured a stray mother cat and kittens the whole time he was here? He didn't like the odds of that. Especially since she still hadn't answered his question.

"I know they can't *all* stay," she said, as if he'd voiced his doubts. "I'll find homes for them. I don't think it'll be hard. Look at them. They're adorable. We've got ranchers with barns all around, if nothing else." As if they'd heard the compliment, three of the kittens slowly poked their heads out of the box. "If I put a flyer up on the church bulletin board, I'll probably have them all spoken for by Friday."

"None of the kittens can leave their mother for eight weeks, not just Charlie." *Stop offering advice*, Neal chided himself.

The three adventurous ones began making their way out of the box to wander around the porch. "Oh, I know," Tessa said. "I got the whole speech from Dr. D. I figure that'll leave me plenty of time to find them homes."

She was already planning. Seriously, the woman's thoughts flashed like a neon sign. Her eyes narrowed, her lips pressed together while her eyebrows scrunched up, and her fingers tapped against the box.

"I can set up one basket out here and another one with a bunch of blankets in the mudroom. They need a litter box, right? And food later when they're done nursing. And bowls for the food and water. Doc gave me a list."

That was it? She just took in eight cats for two months on a moment's notice? With clearly no experience? Before lunch?

Neal was almost grateful when her expression changed. "But wait…" Maybe she was having a few second thoughts about her impulsive decision.

He stood there, waiting for Tessa to dial down her big plans.

"You can't let a kitten go to just anybody, can you?"

Neal had no idea how to answer that.

"I mean, it's a commitment." She rose and walked down the stairs, leaving Neal to corral the kittens away from the steps. "You've got to choose someone who will be caring." She turned back to him. "It's not like a sweater you can return next week because you didn't like the color."

Neal knew all too well there were some decisions you could never go back on. Some choices changed a whole life from the moment they were made.

Tessa hopped back up the porch steps and paced the floorboards as if she'd need to decide on suitable adopters within the hour. "Maddie and Margie Walker might want two—they're twins. And old Mrs. Cooper might love the company if it's not too much for her." Tessa's eyes cast over the porch railing, out toward the street, as if a parade of potential cat owners might just be making its way down her driveway.

Suddenly, Tessa scowled hard enough to make Neal turn to see what had come into view. "Certainly not her."

Neal's stomach dropped a foot at the sour-faced woman who was walking down the street.

Norma Binton. He'd stopped in the pharmacy where she worked behind the counter yesterday, just to watch her. Lurking a distance away while pretending to flip through some of the offerings on the magazine rack. Neal couldn't stop himself from asking, "Why not her?" He forced a casual tone into his words.

"Oh, that's Old Biddy Binton. I don't think she'd know how to be nice—even to a kitten. She's just a mean old woman. No, sir. I don't think I'd give her one of those sweet kittens even if she begged."

Neal swallowed hard. Norma Binton wasn't just some mean old woman who didn't deserve to adopt a poor defenseless kitten.

Norma Binton was his mother.

She just didn't know it yet.

Chapter Three

Tessa managed to wait two whole days before she bothered Neal again about the kittens. When she found him outside washing his car on a sunny Wednesday afternoon, it seemed the perfect time to ask for help.

"Hi," she said as she stood on her side of the driveway their houses shared. "How's the vacation going?" Dumb question.

He looked up from his attention to a headlight. "Um…fine."

She waited for him to ask how Dolly and the kittens were doing. He didn't.

"Dolly and the kittens are doing great," she offered anyway.

"Glad to hear it."

Another pause. Neal wrung out the rag he was holding into the bucket at his feet.

"They're so much fun to watch," she went on, feeling awkward about how the conversation was so one-sided. He'd been easy to talk to the other day—or, at least, that was how she'd perceived it. Maybe she'd really overstepped the boundaries between neighbor and veterinarian. The man was on vacation, after all. Only he was so much nicer than Dr. D, who was becoming a bit of a grump over her many questions. "I'm hardly getting any work done on my writing project because they're just so entertaining."

"They are a cute bunch. And eight is a lot." He began working on the other headlight…the one farther away from her.

She took two steps over to his side of the driveway. "Well, actually, maybe not all of them are doing great. I'm worried about Charlie."

His hand stilled on the car fender and

Tessa wondered if it was from attention or annoyance. "He's so small." She found herself worrying about the little kitten all the time. It was risky how much she was pulling for the kitten to make it, but she couldn't help herself.

"He is." Neal dropped the rag into the soapy water. The tone he gave the two words didn't sound as assuring as she would have liked. "What does Dr. Davidson say about his weight gain?"

"He says he ought to be gaining more. But he *is* gaining." Dr. D kept slipping all kinds of cautionary language into their visits. She knew the words were designed to keep her from getting too invested. Well, that ship had sailed. "Could you... could you just maybe look at him? Just for a minute? Honestly, I think Dr. D's going to stop answering the phone if I call with one more question."

Tessa knew full well she was imposing. Pastor Newton would probably tell her she was fixating on the kitten, projecting all kinds of anxieties about Greg onto the little animal. Still, that was only half of it.

She found herself unable to ignore an out-of-nowhere urge to draw Neal out. The man had spent most of the last two days sitting on his back porch staring into the sunset. His walk was slow and deliberate, as if he continually lugged around a dark cloud of thoughts. She wanted him to see the kittens not only for his professional opinion, but because she hoped they'd lighten whatever load he was carrying. Call it reporter's instinct, but Tessa was convinced Neal Rodgers was either hiding something, wrestling with something or running from something. Whatever the case, she got clear signals he wasn't going to offer it up for conversation.

It was probably a bad sign that he'd waited so long before saying, "Sure."

She gave him a wide, warm smile. "Great. Thanks. Just for a minute."

Relief loosened her chest as Neal followed her up onto her porch and into the mudroom, where the kittens were happily frolicking around in the pen she'd set up for them. "They seem to like the setup," she offered.

He nodded. "You did a good job with it." Neal gingerly stepped over the short octagonal fencing she'd picked up from the hardware store to stand amid the kittens. Dolly eyed him at first, but then seemed to remember him. She didn't protest as he crouched and picked up one of the kittens. "Which one is this?"

"That's Loretta. She's a troublemaker, that one."

Tessa was glad for the small laugh that brought from Neal. "Hello there, Loretta."

Despite his earlier distance, he handled the kittens as if they were important. Precious, even. There wasn't enough of that in the world. The tenderness he showed the animals clashed with the undercurrent of unrest she kept getting off the man.

Neal picked up and inspected each of the kittens, asking their names. He warmed with each minute spent with the animals. By the time he slowly raised Charlie from his spot by Dolly's side, Neal was closer to the man she'd met the other morning.

"He's small," Neal said. "But he's doing okay. Are the other kittens giving him a good chance to nurse?"

Tessa jumped on the chance for conversation. "Oh, he's got some fight in him. Blake tried to nudge him away, but Charlie stands his ground."

Neal returned Charlie to Dolly's side and sat back on his haunches. "That's good. Keep an eye on that."

She was worried he'd leave immediately, but was pleased to see he didn't rush off. "I will. Just a pen full of cuteness, wouldn't you say? I can sit and watch them for hours."

He gave another small laugh as Reba attacked his shoelace as if it were a mortal foe.

She decided to venture a bit further since he wasn't bolting back to his car wash.

"So, when you're not offering pro bono kitty care to your nosy neighbor, what are you doing on this long vacation? A whole month off work sounds positively luxurious, if you ask me."

Neal raised an eyebrow at his neighbor. "Does Valerie fill you in this much on all her vacation renters?"

Tessa shrugged. "She's nice enough to let me know who I'll be living next to. Not if it's a weekend or a few days, but a whole month…" She pushed her hair out of her eyes nervously, and he noticed the unusual clarity of the blue again. "She asked me to be friendly."

Neal stood. "Somehow, I don't think anyone has to *ask* you to be friendly."

"I'll take that as a compliment. Friendly is how we do things here in Wander Canyon. Well, friendly with a strong dose of nosy, but most of us mean well."

"Most?"

"We've got some old hens like most

towns this size. If you haven't gotten a suspicious stare from Biddy Binton at the drugstore, you will."

Old Biddy Binton. There was that nickname again, and it did not promise a good outcome for why he was here. "The lady who walked by the other day?" he asked.

"That's the one. She and a few of her friends poke their noses where they don't belong. Don't take her personally. I'll introduce you around to our friendlier sorts, if you like."

Oh, he had to take Norma Binton personally. Very personally. Or he could just never reveal who he was and walk away. Somehow, Neal wondered if it would take the whole month to make that decision. Stepping out of the kitten pen, he asked, "So she's lived here a long time. Any family?"

"Norma? No. She's been alone as long as I can remember. She's the classic lonely old lady who yells at kids to get off her lawn. She's in church every Sunday—

front pew and everything—but I don't see a lot of Christian kindness in that woman." Tessa opened the door from her mudroom into her kitchen. "Want a cup of coffee?"

Neal wasn't any better at making coffee than he was at cooking a meal. The scent coming from the kitchen lured him against his better judgment. "Sure."

The kitchen looked like a real home kitchen. Bright colors, cheery drapes, bowls lined up on shelves and containers lined up on counters. The space gleamed with sunshine, just like its owner. "So, really," she called as she pulled a pair of mugs down from the shelf, "what are you going to do on your vacation?"

The coffeepot was full and the brew smelled enticingly fresh. She'd had it waiting for him, hadn't she?

Tessa poured two cups and handed one to him. He took a sip and felt the rare urge to offer a compliment. "Good coffee." When had he stopped being so free with praise to people? To his coworkers? Customers?

"You think this is good, make sure you go to The Depot. Molly Bradshaw makes the best coffee in the canyon."

"I'll remember that."

A small pause hung between them before she said, "You seem to spend a lot of time looking out into the mountains."

It bugged him that she knew that. He'd wanted to stay a bit invisible until he knew whether or not to reveal who he was and why he was there.

She caught his reaction. "Sorry. It's just that I can see your porch from this window. It's no business of mine how you spend your time."

And yet here she was, showing him just the opposite. Neal dumped some sugar into his coffee and rubbed the back of his neck with his other hand. "Work's been hectic. I just need to unwind. I don't have any plans, really. Read a lot, I suppose." There were four unopened books on his coffee table. "Take naps." He'd not slept well since his arrival. "Maybe hike up into some of those mountains." That kind of exertion felt beyond him at the moment, but it seemed like the thing you ought to say at the foot of those glorious peaks.

He didn't want to leave, but he needed to get the conversation off himself. "Do you miss him? Your son, I mean."

The personal question—especially from him—seemed to catch her off balance. "Well, now," she said, "that's a tricky question to ask the single mom of a teen-age boy. I miss him to pieces, but I'm grateful for the peace and quiet. And the lower grocery bill. And I don't miss the mountain of laundry one bit."

"How long ago did you split from Greg's father?"

She toyed with the napkin ring on the table where they were sitting. "Four years ago. We were married ridiculously young. Probably too young to know we weren't the best match. If you ask Nick, he'll tell you the split was mutual and very friendly."

Neal gave her a dubious look. "Was it?"

"A marriage takes two people," Tessa responded. "When one person decides to stop holding up their end, there's only so much praying and trying you can do before you just have to make peace with it." She sighed. "So, while we've managed to stay civil, our split wasn't my definition of *mutual*."

"I'm sorry." It seemed like the thing to say.

"Thanks. It's hard, but Greg's worth it. I want him to grow up with a good idea of moms, dads and families. Not enough of that in this world anymore, you know?"

He certainly knew that. "Yeah."

"I'm finding some amazing families and romances in this historical research I'm doing on Wander Canyon. That's my other project—my family history. And the town's. The stories I've found so far are rich enough, I think there are more than a few novels in here."

"You're writing a novel?"

She waved off the idea. "Or maybe just a town history. I don't know. Silly, huh?"

"Maybe not. People have a need to know the stories of their ancestors. There's a big hole when it's missing."

His choice of words caught her attention. "Are your folks gone?"

Now he'd done it. He'd let her questions and coffee and gentle eyes make him talk about more than he should have. *Are your folks gone?* There wasn't a more complex question in the world for Neal.

They were gone, but they weren't. For most of his life, Mom and Dad had been all he'd needed, even when he was old enough to grasp that they weren't his biological parents. And then, about a year ago, something had begun to unravel. The big hole he'd just spoken of had begun to affect him in ways he couldn't explain.

He ran his hands through his hair, not

sure he wanted to get into this but not finding any graceful exit. "It's a tricky business."

Her eyebrows furrowed, so he went on. "I admit, for most people, that's a pretty black-and-white question. But I'm adopted. I don't know much more than that." While that wasn't completely true, Neal wasn't ready to drop the bomb about Norma Binton now, or maybe ever. Not after the way people spoke about the woman.

Curiosity filled Tessa's features, just like he knew it would. "Like Charlie," she said in a way that made him feel foolish and somehow comforted at the same time. As if the kittens hadn't been such a problematic accident.

Maybe it would lift the dark fog he found himself in if he talked about it just a little bit. "I suppose you could put it that way."

"Can't you find out that kind of information now? Are you looking? Is that what your vacation is about?"

"Yes, that information is easy to come by now. But thirty years ago, things weren't that easy. And finding out has to be a two-way street. I can want to find my parents, but if they don't want to be found... Well, it's like you said—there's only so much praying and trying you can do before you just have to make peace with it." Of course, he hadn't done that, had he? He wouldn't be here if he'd made any kind of peace with it.

The compassion he'd seen in her eyes toward the kittens was suddenly trained on him. "Who wouldn't want to know their child? That he'd turned out well and healthy and loved by someone? Who'd say no to a request like that?"

If Neal had to make a list of questions that kept him up at night, those would top his list. "My birth mother, evidently." The words caught thick in his throat. He hadn't dared talk about this to anyone else. It wasn't fair that Tessa's relentless care of the little kitten had cracked open the irrational abandonment he felt.

He didn't like feeling cracked open. When the adoption agency told him his birth mother had declined ever to open communications, it had felt like a slap in the face. As if he were some shameful detail best left swept under the rug.

"That's wrong. I'm sorry."

Neal took a dose of comfort from the indignation in her tone.

Maybe he wasn't cracking open. Maybe he was just peeling off some of the layers he'd built up around himself over all the years. Shedding the protective skin that told him it didn't matter that he'd been adopted. After all, one woman's abandonment had opened the door for another woman's love.

"My adoptive mom is a wonderful woman," he said for himself as much as Tessa. "So is my dad. I went into veterinary medicine because of him—he's a vet, too." The sound of the kittens mewing and playing came from the mudroom next to the kitchen. Neal had forgotten what a happy sound such a thing could be.

"What do your mom and dad think of your search for your birth parents?"

"They don't know," he admitted. "Nobody knows. Well, except you do, now."

"You haven't told them you're looking?"

Neal felt the words come surprisingly easily. Was that a reporter skill, or just the way Tessa was? "They've always told me they'd support me finding out. I just never wanted to. It never really mattered. And then, all of a sudden, this year, it just... started to matter."

"Why?"

Neal gave her the only answer he had. "I don't know. I guess I just couldn't ignore the empty hole anymore."

He watched her investigative instincts kick in. Her eyes narrowed in thought, she pursed her lips together, and you could just see the woman's gears turning. "There have to be a ton of ways to find out, even if she isn't cooperating. What about your birth father? Can he okay the connection?"

Neal wasn't sure it was safe to put Tessa on this path. This was a delicate process, and her intrepid nature could blow the whole thing up in his face. "No dad in the picture. Whoever he was, he was long gone by the time my mother gave birth. That's the only fact I do know."

That wasn't exactly true. Commercial DNA testing could serve up a whole host of facts, if you knew where to look. The test he'd taken had connected him with a third cousin who had said just enough to lead him to Wander Canyon. Tessa wasn't the only person on this porch with investigative skills.

While Neal couldn't be 100 percent certain Norma Binton was his biological mother, he had enough information to confront her and ask. And based on what he'd seen so far, he had little reason to believe any such revelation would have a happy ending. That, among other things, was the reason he spent so much time staring at the mountains wrestling with his disappointment and regret.

Tessa straightened in her chair. "I'll help you."

He hadn't asked for her help. He didn't think he needed it. He wasn't even sure he wanted it. Neal wasn't the least bit sure what he wanted to have happen next. But the simple way she offered her help to him felt too much like the way she'd opened her home to all those kittens. To be swept up in someone's care suddenly felt like a rare gift—even if he had reason to believe he'd regret it later.

The word spilled out of his mouth before he could swallow it back. "Okay."

Chapter Four

"Can we, Mom? Can we?"

That afternoon, Tessa stared at the two little girls as they begged their mother. Marilyn Walker was a good friend, and there was no one she'd like to see two of the kittens go to more than Mari's twin daughters, Margie and Maddie. She leaned in toward the woman as they sat on Tessa's porch swing. She had fixed up a baby gate across the steps so that the kittens could play—supervised, of course—freely on the back porch. "C'mon. You had to know you weren't leaving here without two kittens."

Mari adopted a false scowl. "I *am* leaving here without two kittens. You said yourself they're not old enough to leave their mother."

This, of course, produced a dramatic moan from each of the girls. A twin torrent of pleas for kittens filled the sunny afternoon.

"Don't mince words with a writer, Mari. You knew there was no way you were getting out of this afternoon without *dibs* on two kittens." She pointed down to the two girls sprawled on the porch floor in the sunshine, each one with a kitten tucked adorably against her chest. "I think it's pretty safe to say Reba and Loretta are now spoken for."

Mari raised an eyebrow. "I hadn't noticed." But the corner of her mouth turned up in a way that let Tessa know the deal had been struck.

"Of course, those names are just temporary. When you girls pick out their forever names, I'll start using them so they'll recognize those by the time they come home to you."

Margie fixed her mom with a pleading look. "Are they coming home to us, Mom? Are they?"

Mari knew a losing battle when she saw one. "Yes, I guess they are."

The resulting squeal probably echoed all the way to Neal's house.

Tessa remembered a warning from Neal. "And Wyatt's okay with this, right?" She knew Mari didn't share her husband's impulsive nature, so she had no doubt it had been a joint decision to come here with the girls.

"He said he got to name the kittens, actually."

"Nooooooo!" protested both girls as loudly as their previous squeal.

Mari smiled. "I'm only kidding, girls. Of course you get to name them." She turned to Tessa. "We both know that man would come up with something outrageous if we let him."

"True enough," Tessa answered with a chuckle. Wyatt may have started life as a rebel and Wander Canyon's resident bad boy, but he'd grown into an amazing and loving father to Mari's two girls. Mari and Wyatt were one of Wander's most surprising love stories—and the town boasted quite a few lately. Wyatt loved those twin girls as if they were his own. Tessa thought of all the happiness of that adoptive family, and found herself wondering if Neal had known the same.

Margie hugged the kitten tight and gave Maddie a serious look. "We gotta think hard about names. They have to be perfect."

"You'll come up with the right ones, I'm sure," Tessa said as her heart filled with satisfaction. Counting Charlie, three of the seven kittens had homes now. Four more to go. "After all, names are important."

"Speaking of important things, how's that history project of yours coming?"

Mari asked. "Happily digging in with all this spare time?"

Tessa nodded back toward the pile of old documents on her desk in the study window behind them. "Spare time? These little guys keep me busy." She sighed. "But I'm making a little progress. At least on the research, if not on the writing. Based on what I've found so far, I'm not sure if I have a history or a Wild West novel in there."

Mari gave a smirk. "Quiet little Wander Canyon?"

"Let's just say quiet little Wander Canyon hasn't always been so quiet. I've only just started digging, but I'm already seeing threads of some major drama when you go back a generation or two." Tessa chose her words carefully, aware that Mari's family went back in the canyon almost as far as her own family.

"Oh, I'm not surprised. We've seen some pretty major drama recently, and

I like to think we're more civilized than some of our ancestors."

Mari had the right to say that—some of that drama had been in her own family. The girls' father, Mari's late husband, had been the source of a great deal of pain just when Mari's current husband, Wyatt, came into the picture. Tessa had watched Wyatt's love transform both Mari and her girls. While her split from Nick hadn't been nearly as dramatic, Tessa longed for someone to transform her own life.

She gazed at the beautiful wedding ring gracing Mari's left hand. *Promise me I'll find love again, will You, Lord?* That felt like an immature request to make of God—He wasn't some vending machine you could pull a lever and have your wishes granted. But she was sure God knew her heart, and her heart was lonely. Content, but lonely.

Tessa must have let her eyes wander toward the house next door, because Mari nudged her with a knowing look. "Yvonne said your new neighbor came into the bakery the other day. She made a point of telling me how handsome he was. Charming, too, in a soft-spoken kind of way."

Handsome, charming and *soft-spoken* were good adjectives for Neal. But he was also a bit sullen, sad, and seemed to have a lot on his mind. Based on what he'd told her, he was indeed wrestling with some big issues. "He's certainly a better neighbor than the gaggle of bridesmaids in here the other weekend. Sometimes it's fun to live next to a vacation rental. Other times, not so much."

"Yvonne said he's here for a whole month?"

Tessa wondered how it was that Yvonne Walker—Mari's sister-in-law and the town baker—was more able to wring details out of customers than many of Tessa's own newspaper interviews. "Maybe I should start using Yvonne as a news source," she joked.

"Is he looking to move here?" Mari

asked as she picked up the mother cat and began stroking her until a velvety purr came from the animal. Mari had a mother's heart in so many ways.

"He says he's on vacation." Tessa sighed. "I wonder what it's like to take a month-long vacation. Must be lovely."

"At least you've got three weeks of peace and quiet with Greg gone. How's he doing? How are you doing?"

Tessa opted for honesty. "He's having a ball. Clearly, Dad is way more fun than Mom. I feel like I'm going to get a wild animal back from Utah just in time to stuff him into the ninth grade."

"Well, at least you'll have had practice with wild kittens."

"They're cuter. And they definitely eat less. But I do miss Greg." She dared to voice the thought that had kept her up last night. "There's a tiny part of me scared I'll get a call at the end of the summer telling me Greg's decided high school in Utah is a better adventure than high school in Wander Canyon."

Mari put an understanding hand on Tessa's arm. "He won't do that."

"I don't know," Tessa admitted. "Nick's taken him to three theme parks already. Greg's off with Mr. Fun Dad while I'm content spending hours in the library on my week off. What does that make me?"

Mari squeezed Tessa's arm. "It makes you a mom tired from doing all the heavy lifting. From being a parent, not a playmate."

Tessa was surprised by the lump in her throat. She swallowed hard, trying to tamp down the fear that Greg could be slipping away from her. Spending almost a month with Nick was a good thing for Greg. She wanted him to have a relationship with his father beyond phone calls, weekend visits, and presents that usually took the form of gift cards arriving at the last minute through FedEx.

Mari's eyes told Tessa she hadn't hidden her feelings well. "Greg knows who he can depend on. Nick may be a barrel of fun, but Greg knows how much you love him and will always be there for him. Someone once told me that kids—even teenagers—are far smarter about that sort of thing than we ever give them credit for."

It was advice Tessa had given Mari not a month ago when the girls were giving their mom a hard time. "Who told you that?" she asked, glad to feel a small laugh replace the large lump in her throat.

"You did. And it's true. It was right to let him go spend time with Nick, and your son will come home a better young man on account of it."

"He'll be fifteen by the time he comes back to me. That's old enough to get a learning permit." One of the hardest parts of letting Greg go was knowing he'd spend his birthday away from her. Turning fifteen seemed so important.

As they were talking, Neal came out of

his garage with a tool kit in one hand and a box of cans and towels in the other. After a short wave to Tessa, he set down the items and popped the hood on his snazzy blue convertible. A month off and a fancy car to tinker with—the man's life couldn't be more different from her daily scramble. Her life was a boring, used-SUV existence.

Tessa hoped Mari didn't take too much notice of the way Neal filled out the dark shirt he wore, or the *don't even realize how good I look* way he moved around the vehicle.

"You need to make sure you have something fun to do on Greg's birthday. You know, a distraction?" Mari waggled her eyes on the last word, nodding in Neal's direction. "And I don't mean kittens."

Tessa had to admit, her new neighbor was a distraction. And a rather nice one at that. She'd sincerely meant her offer to help him find his birth mother—it seemed like such a compelling puzzle to solve.

Tessa was warming to the idea that it was no accident this man in search of information had moved in next to a woman whose favorite thing to do was to find things out. "I hadn't thought about it. I just sort of planned to muddle through. Maybe with a pint of ice cream and a sappy movie." The words sounded embarrassingly pathetic as she said them aloud. She'd once been known as a woman with admirable spunk. Where was all that spunk now?

"So you totally forgot the church barbecue was that night?"

"No, I just didn't want to go all by myself. That didn't seem like the night to get a front-row seat to all that family happiness."

Mari fixed Tessa with a no-nonsense glare. "Who says you have to go all by yourself? I mean, what better way to thank a man for helping you with kittens than to feed him barbecue?"

Even though she'd already invited Neal in for coffee, asking him to go to the barbecue seemed…forward. Risky. "I don't know. He keeps giving off 'I want to be left alone' vibes."

"Didn't you just tell me he likes your coffee? So, you've had him over for coffee. Come on, Tessa. You're braver than that. Ask him. If he says no, then he says no."

"Tell you what," Tessa said. "If the right opportunity presents itself, I'll ask."

"Well," Mari said with a wink, "now I know what to pray for."

Neal had to give Wander Canyon one thing: the town did boast terrific coffee.

His one morning at Tessa's had shown him that the jar of instant coffee in the rental didn't cut it anymore. So, based on Tessa's recommendation, he'd decided to reinstate his morning jog on Thursday morning in the direction of The Depot, the old-time train car that had become a coffee bar, and likely served something better than his usual toaster breakfast by a long shot.

He'd given this morning's run a second purpose as well. Neal timed his run with the opening of the drugstore. It gave him a chance to watch Norma Binton make her slow, slumped saunter down Main Street to her job behind the counter there. He stopped to watch her even longer, peering out of the corner of his eye as he bent on the pretense of tying his shoe.

Am I looking at my mother?

His fascination with the possibility continually warred with the fear that she was. Norma Binton was such a bitter clash to the illogical fantasy he'd built up around the mysterious woman who'd given him life. Neal wasn't sure there ever was such a thing as a mean-old-lady walk, but there was definitely something mean in how Norma moved through the world.

His parents had molded him into who he was, but could he escape his ancestry? He didn't want to end up some mean-old-man version of her. That hole in his life, in his past, had soured him lately, and this trip was supposed to do something about it.

As Norma pulled open the door to the drugstore and lumbered in, Neal straightened, pulled in a deep breath of mountain air and set his feet in the direction of The Depot. *She is who you let her be. No more—or no less. Figure out what you want from this before you go trying to get it.*

Neal asked himself what he wanted as he continued his run until he landed at the steps of The Depot. He'd hoped to get a good cup of coffee and a cinnamon Danish. What he also found was Tessa.

Chapter Five

Tessa was seated in one of the booths at The Depot, having an animated conversation with a man and a young boy. She laughed at something the boy said, and Neal remembered how much he liked that sound.

Tessa had offered small laughs in their conversations, but this was a full, open laugh that rang pleasantly in his ears. The kittens evidently made her laugh a lot, the sound of it often wafting through his windows to interrupt his quiet. He ought to have minded, but he didn't. She had one of those infectious laughs you could hear clear across a room—or a yard—and he found himself smiling a bit whenever he heard it, including now.

Tessa caught his eye and smiled. Immediately, she waved him over. "Neal! When you get your order, come meet Jake and Cole."

Tessa was clearly intent on delivering on her offer to introduce Neal around town.

He paid for his order and grabbed a napkin in one hand and his drink in the other. "Hello," he said, wiping his beading forehead. The sun came strong this far up the mountains, and his adjustment to the altitude was still making him work hard. "I'm probably a bit too sweaty to make a good first impression."

The man looked at Neal's shoes. "A runner."

"Used to be," he panted, his words still sounding winded. "Trying to be again. The altitude's still messing with me."

"Any chance you play baseball?"

"Badly," Neal answered. "And I'm only here for a month's vacation."

"We're not picky," the man replied. "We can't afford to be."

Tessa smiled. "Jake here is captain of our community baseball team. Which means he never stops recruiting."

Jake smiled as well. "Which means we'll take anybody. For any amount of time."

Neal wanted to know more about Wander Canyon, but he wasn't sure he was ready to get that deep into Norma's hometown community. He took a sip of coffee. "Afraid I'll have to take a pass."

"Dr. Rodgers is a veterinarian," Tessa said to the young boy. "Maybe you can ask him about your turtles."

Before he could draw a breath to explain that reptiles were generally the clients of exotic breed vets, Cole looked up at him and launched into a detailed question about how long it took turtle eggs to hatch.

Jake offered an apologetic smirk. "We

thought we'd taken steps to avoid turtle romance, but eggs appeared in the tank two days ago. It's been a bit awkward."

"I want baby turtles," Cole insisted. "I wanna see them hatch. Do we hafta help the mommy turtle?"

"I was about to tell them to come over and ask you, and look at that—here you are," Tessa said.

He wasn't sure about the significance Tessa seemed to place on the coincidence. "The coffee here is as good as you said."

"Yeah, Molly keeps the whole town caffeinated. I'm sure you'll become a regular."

Neal guessed Molly to be the friendly woman behind the counter, but he had never been a "regular" enough at any establishment to do something like learn a server's name. Given why he was here, now wasn't the time to start, either.

"Neal's been a big help with the kittens." Tessa made it sound heroic.

"Tessa's doing a fine job. Dr. Davidson

ought to be proud of her." The resulting glow in Tessa's eyes shouldn't have gotten to him the way it did.

"I'm proud of my mama and daddy turtle. But Dr. D says he can't help me." Neal thought that was no answer to give a little boy, but he wasn't about to call this Dr. Davidson out on how he ran his practice.

You're not in Wander Canyon to get involved.

Tessa's face told him she wasn't too happy with how Dr. D had treated the boy, either. "I figured *you* could do better than that," she said.

Neal ran a hand across his chin. Maybe he could just be a little bit involved. "Well, now, turtles are a specialty not many of us vets know. I've never treated one myself." The fall in the little boy's eager features wouldn't let him walk away at just that. So, even though he figured this might fall into a category of more than a little bit involved, he heard himself reply, "But I could do some research and get back to you. Would that be okay?"

Cole's bobbing nod of approval was as cute as any of Tessa's kittens.

"I'd appreciate that," Jake said. "We don't want to mess this up. Cole, say thanks to Dr. Rodgers."

"Thanks, Dr. Rodgers!" came the enthusiastic reply. The boy fixed Neal with a happy look. "Have you seen the turtle on the carousel? He's my favorite."

"I'm sure Dr. Rodgers has seen our carousel," Tessa replied. She turned to look up at him, and Neal felt his stomach drop. "You have seen the carousel, haven't you?" She pointed to a building not fifty yards away, with its brightly colored sign above the large double doors reading Wander Canyon Carousel of Happiness. The doors, of course, were open.

There weren't going to be too many ways to duck out of this. Neal was certain he was going to regret it when he answered, "Not yet."

Sure enough, the answer launched Cole immediately out of his seat. "You gotta. Right now." The boy grabbed one of Neal's hands and one of Jake's hands and began tugging. "Come on, Dad. Let's show him. There's a turtle and a octopus and a porcupine and all sorts of stuff."

Neal threw a last-ditch *help me* look Tessa's way. Her amused eyes gave a conspiratorial sparkle as she stood to join the fun. She clearly thought this was a great idea, even grabbing his coffee to trot happily behind them.

"It is fun," she called as Cole continued to tug the two men toward the door as if this were the best idea he'd ever had. "Even for grown-ups. If you ask me, it's a big part of what makes Wander Canyon special."

Neal didn't know why she was continuing her sales pitch. Cole was doing a pretty good job of ensuring he saw this carousel.

Jake wasn't far behind. "No Wander

Canyon visit is complete without it." He checked his watch. "And it just opened ten minutes ago."

As if to announce its own importance, the sound of calliope music came in through the train car window. "I guess I can go see it."

"Oh, no, you don't just *see* it," countered Jake, who seemed to be enjoying this as much as Cole. "You ride. Everybody rides."

Ride? As in get on one of those ponies and go around? "Thanks all the same, but I don't think I'll ride."

"Oh, that's what everyone says—*at first*." Tessa darted past the men and backed into the door to push it open despite the coffee in each hand. Her expression was one of delighted victory. The way she'd been talking about showing him around the small town, Neal had no doubt that was how she viewed the moment.

"Seriously," Jake said. "You hadn't noticed the giant carousel in the middle of town?"

In fact, Neal must have passed it several times. How many towns had a carousel on Main Street? It bothered him that he was always too absorbed in his thoughts to notice something so unique. Special, even.

They entered the large barnlike building that housed the amusement. Neal could see the carousel churning around just beyond the ticket taker's booth. Cole wasn't kidding—the thing really did have a crazy assortment of animals.

"It is kind of a veterinarian's carousel, now that I think about it," Tessa offered.

"Or a zookeeper's," Neal replied, pleasantly surprised he'd made something close to a joke. Even his own mother had begun to remark about how he'd lost his sense of humor. The carousel's most unique feature came to him after a moment. "No ponies?"

"Not a one," Jake said. "Just about everything else, though." He pulled a five-dollar bill out of his pocket and handed it to the grandmotherly lady behind the counter.

Neal balked. "You're not paying for me to ride, are you?"

"Here in Wander, it's a tradition that a visitor never pays for their own first ride. Pauline here would have my hide if she found out I didn't spring for it."

"Welcome to Wander Canyon," said Pauline, presenting four tickets as if they were carnival prizes.

"Now you've got to," Tessa said with a wink. "Really, it's more fun than you think. Come on."

Neal felt downright ridiculous as they walked into the large round enclosure. Cole shot straight to the turtle as promised. Jake chose a wildly colored rooster. "Which one for you?" Neal asked Tessa, suddenly curious as to her favorite.

"Oh, I've ridden them all." She set the to-go coffee cups on a side railing. "I'll just pick the one next to whichever you choose."

It felt like an absurd task—choosing which animal to ride. He was too old to be riding a merry-go-round. And yet the three other families also boarding the ride seemed to think it was a perfectly normal thing to do. Lost for an appropriate choice, Neal pointed to a golden lion just behind Cole's turtle.

"Oh, good choice," Tessa said as she made straight for the fleecy white sheep beside the lion. "This is one of my favorites."

As he made to climb onto the animal, Neal was halted by the sight of Jake helping Cole onto his turtle. With tender care, Jake hoisted his son up onto the shiny green turtle shell and secured the leather safety strap. A sharp thought speared into Neal's chest without warning. *That could have been me. I could have had memories of my family taking me for rides on this carousel.*

It made no sense. He had many happy memories with his adoptive parents. He had no reason to feel the loss of this one instance. He wasn't even 100 percent sure Norma was his biological mother. Or if she'd even lived here when she'd given birth to him. None of those facts did anything to lessen the out-of-nowhere sting that overtook him watching Cole and Jake.

Tessa mistook his hesitation. "Hey, look, you don't have to if you really don't want to."

"No," Neal countered, hurrying to swing his leg over the lion and grab the pole despite how silly it felt. "I'll ride."

The happy music swelled up to clash in his ears as the carousel platform began to turn.

Tessa's laugh made him smile, but it didn't quite drown out the off-kilter sensation of being on the carousel. He couldn't take his eyes off the memory-making exchange of looks happening between Cole and Jake. As if Wander Canyon was the best place on earth to grow up.

But he hadn't grown up here. He was only back to discover everything he'd missed. And that felt like a wound even the most skilled doctor couldn't stitch up.

Tessa watched Neal as the lion bobbed up and down. Most adults were embarrassed at first, but soon enjoyed the ride no matter how silly it seemed. Something else entirely was going on with Neal.

His hands gripped the pole so tight, his knuckles paled. She expected him to glance at her, to make some goofy remark about adults riding a carousel, or to at least look around and enjoy the spectacle that was the Wander carousel. He stared at Jake and Cole, but at the same time, his vision seemed far away. As if he wanted to be there, but could barely stand being there.

It took her half the ride before her brain connected the dots. There wasn't anything more iconic about Wander Canyon than this carousel. Neal's discomfort wasn't about the carousel; it was about being here. Neal wasn't just on a vacation to think through the discovery of a birth mother. He was here to *find* his birth mother. In Wander Canyon. Neal's birth mother was here. She had lived—or was still living—in Wander Canyon.

They finished the ride without speaking. Neal gave a cursory thank-you to Jake and Cole, but still looked as if he'd been blindsided. She was grateful she'd set both their coffees aside together, as it gave her a chance to catch him before he headed out of the building behind a gleeful Jake and Cole.

"Hey," she said as she handed him the drink. "Are you okay?"

"Fine," he said.

"No offense, but you are so *not* fine. I'm sorry. If I had known..."

He waved her apology off. "I'm fine. I just...well... The thing is so...*happy.*"

He said it as if the cheer of the place ran him through. That made sense, didn't it? She'd always been so proud of the carousel. Grateful that she'd grown up in Wander Canyon riding it dozens of times and especially on her birthday—children always rode free on their birthdays.

What would it be like to ride it as an adult and be struck by all the rides you'd missed? "I'm sorry," she repeated, not knowing what else to say. She tried to hand him his coffee, but he still stared at the ride. Or not at the ride—the man's gaze seemed a million miles off. Somewhere in a memory—or the lack of one.

"It's not you. It's…" Rather than finish the thought, Neal started walking toward the exit.

Tessa raced after him, the coffees still in each hand spilling a bit from her quick steps. "Hey," she called, then, "Sit down for a minute, will you?" when he didn't slow the first time. If there was one thing the mother of a teenager could do, it was fix someone with a *do as you're told* glare, and she gave Neal her best.

He stilled, glared back, but lowered himself to the bench on the clearing in front of the carousel house. Tessa handed him his coffee, then took a sip of her own. Neal clearly needed to simmer down a bit before she could ask him the question burning in her brain.

When the anxiety stopped radiating off him like a furnace, she pivoted to face him. "She's here, isn't she?" She tried to make her words gentle but insistent, the way Pastor Newton was so good at doing. The reverend could always make people talk about things they didn't want to discuss but needed to. It didn't take a pastoral collar to know Neal was choking on everything he was trying to hold back.

When he didn't refute her, Tessa pressed a bit further. "This isn't just a vacation to think about it. You're here to find her. And you're here in Wander Canyon because *she's* here." When Tessa had told Mari that

Wander Canyon was full of dramatic histories, she'd had no idea how right she'd been.

She chose to wait out his answer. The admission was going to cost him a lot—this wasn't the kind of thing anyone blurted out with ease. *Send me grace,* she prayed as the silence stretched between them. Only it wasn't silence. They could both still hear the cheerful calliope music and children's laughter floating out of the building they'd just left.

Pastor Newton talked about holy moments, places in a life where big things happened, where people opened up and lives shifted. This looked like it might be one of those for Neal. Pastor Newton always said it was a privilege to stand witness to one. Tessa let that sense of honor fuel her patience and plea for grace.

"I don't know for sure," he finally said. Worry drew his words taut. "I'm not sure I want to know."

"Of course you'd want to know," she

replied, then realized the foolishness of that answer. After all, she'd always known her parents were wonderful people. Her freckles and laugh came from her mother. She had her father's dimples, and she and Greg both shared Dad's unruly hair. History was always an affirmation, never a lurking unknown. "It'd be better to know, wouldn't it?" she amended. "I mean, won't you always wonder if you don't?"

"I had a great childhood. My parents were wonderful to me. I owe them everything. Why do I feel like I have to hunt after this?" He met her eyes for the first time since he'd climbed onto the lion. "What's the point of looking for pain?"

What was behind his certainty that this was going to end in pain? "Because maybe it won't. Sure, I get it might be complicated and messy at first, but at least you'll know."

"Maybe I don't need to know."

"Neal, I haven't known you for that long, but even I can see that you need to know. The thing that's eating at you now, I can't see how it will go away by itself. If you know that she's here, then you've got to be close enough to know who she is. Or might be."

Neal set the coffee cup down without having drunk from it and ran his hands over his thighs. He was practically swaying from the weight of it all.

"You know, don't you? Who she is."

Neal didn't say a word, but the way his body tensed told Tessa the answer. What must that be like? Walking around a town, seeing someone who had such a massive impact on your life, playing total stranger when you were anything but? The dark cloud he dragged around behind him made total sense now.

Curiosity flooded through her. Any reporter's appetite for mysteries would be salivating at a story like this. A novel plot was literally playing out before her eyes.

Life had taught her, however, that pain unearthed itself with secrets. Sometimes they came out with joy. She'd helped her friend Molly find the dark secret that had driven her now fiancé, Sawyer, to Wander Canyon. That had been a painful path. It had ended in joy, to be sure, but the happy couple had walked a long and tangled path to find each other. Mari knew the cost of secrets as well.

"Have you seen her?"

"Yes." Tessa tried to imagine what that must feel like—to be so near and so far away at the same time. Excruciating.

His attitude told her the answer to this next question, but she asked it anyway. "But you don't like what you've seen?"

Neal managed only the smallest shake of his head. And at the same time, the gesture was enormous. So far beyond disappointment, it made Tessa's heart ache.

She thought about how short she'd been with the grocery store clerk the other day when Greg had left in such a huff. She'd been as mean as Old Biddy Binton, and to someone whom she'd barely known.

"What if you just don't know her? You can't be sure what you see now is what she's truly like, right?"

And there it was...the door Mari had said she'd be praying for. It swung as wide open in front of her as the carousel barn door was behind her. "You need to come to the church barbecue with me Wednesday night."

Neal's head swiveled around to stare at her as if she'd just suggested the most ridiculous thing ever.

It wasn't. It was a brilliant idea. "No, really. Everybody in town comes. It's one of the nicest nights of the whole year. You could even talk to her. It wouldn't look odd—everybody talks to everyone that night. You're just going on appearances right now, and no one should get judged by that."

The hum of tension started to leave him. "So you're saying nosy neighbors in pink fuzzy socks who drag you out of bed at sunrise might be nice people after all."

A glow of purpose filled Tessa's chest. "If you get to know them."

"But what if they turn out to just be nosy, slightly crazy neighbors?" The warmth of his eyes reflected the gentle tease of his words.

"There's really only one way to know for sure. Come on, Neal. Say you'll go. You'll be doing us both a favor. It's Greg's birthday that night and I need a distraction. Your mystery is as good a diversion as they come. Plus—" she waggled her eyebrows playfully "—barbecue."

"Well, when you put it that way…"

Tessa grinned. She'd done it. She'd convinced him to go. Would she feel the same pride if Neal regretted coming to the barbecue? If seeing his birth mother made things far worse instead of better?

There was only one way to find out.

Chapter Six

Tessa sat staring at her phone screen beside her plate of uneaten dinner Saturday evening. *Don't read more into this than is there*, she told herself. *He's a teenager. Teenagers don't think about anyone else's feelings.*

They had agreed to talk by phone on Saturday before dinnertime once a week. Tessa had made the arrangement so she could stay in regular touch with Greg. She was also looking to see if Nick could be conscientious about helping Greg keep that promise. As a family, they were about to enter into the white-water rapids of high school and college. Tessa was looking for reassurances that she and Nick could handle small co-parenting challenges like this before the bigger ones arrived.

She'd waited an hour past the designated call time, even though it felt like a dozen hours. After ninety minutes had gone by, she sent a short text. Hey, it's time. Call? It took three drafts to keep the four words from sounding like nagging.

No response came.

Don't call Nick, she lectured herself. *You'll just get into it with him, and that will make it worse.*

Tessa made double-sure the phone wasn't set on silent before she slipped it into her pocket. She walked over to the kittens' pen and peered in. "How about a little cuteness overload? I could use a distraction here."

While sleeping kittens were adorable, she couldn't seem to find them entertaining. She was too irritated to find Dolly's gentle purring soothing, although the mama cat did look up at her with big green eyes.

"Enjoy it," she said to Dolly. "They need you now. Pretty soon you're just a person who both embarrasses them and fills the refrigerator." When Dolly blinked, Tessa added, "And one does not make up for the other, just in case you were wondering."

I'm discussing parenting with cats, she thought to herself. *How many steps is that away from crazy cat lady?*

The house felt too quiet tonight. Sitting at the kitchen table on a Saturday night waiting for Greg to keep his promise to call made her feel old and lonely. This break was supposed to make her feel young and purposeful again. Short of feline rescue, where was that purpose? It loomed just out of reach, unexplored like the stack of notebooks on her study desk that she passed on her way out to the swing on the back porch.

A chill had come up as the sun was going down, and Tessa grabbed one of

Greg's innumerable hoodies from a wall hook in the mudroom. It felt needy to put it on, rather than the cardigan sweater of hers hanging right next to the hoodie, but she did anyway.

I didn't expect to miss him this much, Lord, she prayed as she settled into the swing, pulling up her knees and wrapping the big sweatshirt fully around her like a blanket. Her mind called up the vision of the small white onesies he'd worn as a baby. The itty-bitty socks and enthralling tiny toes. How it took his whole hand to grip her thumb and how often he'd reached for her. The sweet *I need you* of his four-year-old hand in hers walking down the street to buy a coloring book or some small trinket at Redding's General Store. When had he grown large enough to fill out something she could curl her whole body inside?

Don't make this a test. Don't make it mean more than it does. It's just a phone call. You tell him to make his bed every morning and he doesn't do that, does he?

Try as she might, Tessa couldn't make herself see this call as just a call. This was her assurance—or right now, lack of assurance—that he wouldn't forget her. That the nonstop carnival of fun Nick seemed to have planned for Greg wouldn't lure him away from her.

Tessa pulled the phone from her pocket and stared at the unanswered text. She set the phone next to her on the swing, telling herself she didn't want to miss the ring when it happened.

Greg had dismissed a thousand other small requests in the past year, but this felt big. This was the beginning of that necessary "pulling away" every mother dreaded. There were mothers in the Solos single parents' Bible study at church who told horror stories. Kids who didn't gently pull away, but instead yanked with all their might. Estrangements. Acting out. Harsh words, dumb antics, and even crimes. Drugs, alcohol…

"Just call!" Tessa yelled at the phone before her thoughts went any further down that catastrophic road.

Although every sensible bone in her body cautioned against it, she picked up the phone and typed What happened to our 5pm call?

The phone rang ten seconds later. "Mo-o-o-m." Greg drew the word out in supreme irritation. "I didn't think you really meant that." Background noise and the unsteady focus of his voice told her he was out somewhere. Having too much fun to call his mother.

"I did, actually." Tessa nearly winced at her own words. She tried to save things by brightening her voice to "Sounds like you're having fun."

"Hey, guys," Greg called on the other end of the line, "I'll catch up with you in a minute, just as soon as I get off the phone with my mom." He made it sound like the dreariest of tasks, his tone stinging in her ears.

"Don't let me keep you." She wanted to mean it, but nothing was further from the truth. "New friends?" Maybe he'd give her just a bit of time if she asked about these new friends.

"Okay, great. Yeah, gotta go."

Tessa started to say "I love you," but the connection ended before she could get all the words out. He'd been gone one week and already he didn't have time for her.

The quiet and solitude of the next ten minutes pulled her down like an undertow. Greg's dismissal—even if he didn't mean it that way, she couldn't escape how she felt dismissed—made the house cavernous and the sky too big to care. There were days parenting felt like throwing yourself against a cactus, inviting a thousand tiny pricks to wound you. Today those pricks felt like battle-axes.

He cares, Tessa reassured herself. *He's*

just being a teenage boy. Deep down, he knows.

None of that stopped the sorry-for-my-self tears that stole down her cheeks. And while it should have made her feel better to wipe them on Greg's hoodie wrapped around her, it only really made it worse.

Neal put down his book at the sound. He wasn't even sure what the sound was, only noticing it because of the tiny alarm it set off in the back of his mind.

Laying the book on the table, he moved closer to the window. He angled himself to see outside without being seen, cautious for no real reason.

Sniff. Shaky breath. Small sob. Crying.

Something in his chest pulled tight at the realization that someone was crying—or maybe trying not to cry—and that some-one was Tessa.

Neal shifted his body so that he could see Tessa's porch just in time to watch her wipe her eyes with the floppy sleeve of a gray sweatshirt.

If he went out there, it wouldn't be a short conversation. It wouldn't be light, pleasant neighborly talk. They'd already grown closer than he felt comfortable with, and fear that this would only take them deeper down that path glued his feet to the kitchen's faded yellow linoleum tiles.

She tried to be there for you. You can't just sit here and let her cry out there all by herself. You haven't become that much of a jerk, have you?

Another swallowed sob escaped her and he felt it in his gut. *It's not like you have somewhere you need to be.* Where he needed to be, if he was man enough to admit it, was up on that porch trying to be as much of a friend to her as she had been to him.

Neal couldn't decide if it was chivalry or practicality that had him grab the box of tissues off his coffee table before he headed out the door. It likely didn't matter.

Tessa didn't notice him at first, but when his footsteps crunched on the gravel beside her driveway, she nearly shrank down inside the sweatshirt. A mournful "oooh" floated out from underneath the pile of gray fleece.

"Are you okay in there?" It was a foolish question. Of course she wasn't anything close to all right.

"I'm fine." She sniffled as she tried to sink down farther onto the porch swing.

Neal had to laugh at that. "You are so not fine," he said, echoing her words to him just the other day.

That brought her slightly out from underneath the hooded sweatshirt.

It was large and masculine...probably Greg's. Perhaps that was a hint to her tears. Was she missing her son? The poignancy of that, given his current quest, pressed on him. He wondered—a bit sourly—if Greg knew how fortunate he was to have a mother's love that strong.

Neal walked up the steps and held out the box of tissues. She shook the floppy sleeve until her hand reached out to take the box. "It's silly."

"I doubt that." Tessa was emotional, maybe, but it never seemed to be over anything he'd classify as silly. "Is it Greg?" he ventured.

She picked up the phone and slid it into one of the hoodie's cavernous pockets, an unspoken invitation to sit down. It felt oddly close to sit on the swing with her, but it would be too awkward to decline her gesture. Neal sat, taking care to ensure there was a good amount of space between them. He'd had more than one pet owner collapse in tears onto his shoulder over a dying pet, and such instant intimacy was never his strong suit. If Tessa began sobbing on his shoulder, it wouldn't be good.

"He's a teenager," she moaned, yanking a tissue from the box and blowing her nose. "Clueless is how they come, right?" She sighed. "He didn't mean it. Or, at least, I hope he didn't mean it."

"What did he do?"

Tessa emerged a little bit more from her fleecy burrow. "It's more like what he *didn't* do. As in call. At the time we agreed—or, at least, I thought we'd agreed—that he'd check in."

"Oh." That sounded like something sure to wound a mother missing her son.

She waved the tissue around as she spoke. "And when I stupidly texted him to remind him he was supposed to call me, he answered as if it were the biggest inconvenience on planet Earth."

Ouch.

"Too busy having the time of his life to call his mom. I should be happy he's so happy." Her final words held the threat of more tears.

"I suppose so, but in my experience, it never seems to work that way with moms."

Neal relaxed into the swing, gently rocking it with his feet that were touching the
floor since she was curled up into a little
ball on the other end. For a moment, she
reminded him of the kittens, all curled and
vulnerable. "I remember getting a similar lecture from my mother while I was
at college. It wasn't ever deliberate. More
like a self-centered, didn't-even-think-of-
it kind of thing."

Her chin rose. "Intellectually, I get it. I
do." The hand holding the wadded-up tissue fell to her chest, as if she could touch
the heartache. "Emotionally, his tone...
Ugh." She looked at him with wide, wet
eyes. "When I told him we'd agreed he'd
call on Saturday at five, do you know he
actually said 'You meant that?' As if I
go around saying things I don't mean? To
him? It's like he hates that I need him and
he certainly doesn't need me."

A tear brimmed over her eye to run
down one blotchy cheek, and she swiped

at it with the sweatshirt sleeve despite the full box of tissues at her side.

"He needs you." It felt strange and potent to say such a thing. "He just doesn't know how to show it." That was making an assumption he had no business making. Like the promises he was trained never to make as a veterinarian. Why was it Tessa pulled things out of him he didn't want exposed?

"He tolerates me. Barely. Especially now that he's in the clutches of his incredibly fun and mostly irresponsible father." Her rising temper drove her out of the sweatshirt until she was sitting upright and turned toward him. "I asked Nick to make sure he called me at the agreed time. I don't think Nick was even in the room. I don't even know where Greg was when he was supposed to be calling me." She fixed him with a wounded glare. "Why is it so hard to keep a promise? One call a week? That's all I asked of him. One call."

Asking a teenager to call on a Saturday night seemed a bit of a high bar, but he surely wasn't going to raise that point now. "How many calls has he missed?"

That took some of the wind out of her sails. "Just this one. The first one. So not a great start."

Neal stifled a laugh. He knew she was hurt and unable to see Greg's mistake with any sense of perspective. "You said it yourself. Teenage boys are clueless. Totally focused on themselves and the moment. It really could be that this isn't about how he feels about you. I've never been a parent. And I get that you're hurt. But I don't think he hurt you. Or meant to." Neal ran a hand through his hair, sure he was botching this attempt to make her feel better. "Didn't you ever blow off your mom at his age?"

"Never," she countered so dramatically Neal had to raise a doubtful eyebrow. "Well, okay," she relented, "maybe a few times. All of which I deeply regret at the moment."

Her tearful seriousness was—he didn't like how this word kept coming to mind about Tessa—adorable. Sweet and sentimental, but with an admirable bit of spunk and spine behind it. Neal could not ever remember applying such gooey words to any woman, much less one he'd known for less than a week.

"I don't want to spend these three weeks staring at my phone waiting for Greg to call. I want to enjoy this time as much as he is. Well, close to."

"Didn't you tell me you had a writing project you wanted to be working on? A family history?"

"Town history, actually. But my family's all in that history, so it's some of my family history, too. I haven't done any work on it yet."

That seemed an easy solution. "Maybe if you dive into it, you won't be so worried about Greg." He'd picked up the local newspaper and read some of her articles. "You're a good writer."

The compliment lit up her eyes. "You read our paper?"

"Seemed like the thing to do." He didn't need to mention that he was scanning it for information about Norma.

Tessa pulled in a big breath. "You're right. Greg spending this time with his dad was my idea. I wanted him to have fun. Why should I be upset that I got what I wanted? I wouldn't want him to be sitting bored in Utah, wishing he was home. And he's not."

"That's the spirit. Be happy he's having too good a time to remember to call."

She narrowed her eyes and pointed at him. "Now, *that's* going too far. I want him to have a good time *and* remember to call."

Neal got an idea. "What if you set yourself a weekly writing goal to meet by the time he's supposed to call? You know, number of pages written, research books read, that sort of thing. Then you'll have something to tell him when he does call.

And you'll be too busy to worry about him."

"A mom is never too busy to worry," she declared. "But you're right. Thanks."

Neal smiled, suddenly in no hurry to leave the swing with her by his side. "Just being neighborly."

Chapter Seven

Tessa Kennedy must have superpowers. Not the comic book kind, but the persuasion kind. That was the only reason short of the Hand of the Almighty—which was a distinct possibility—that Neal found himself slipping into the back pew at Wander Canyon Community Church the following morning.

Not that Tessa hadn't asked. And suggested. And dropped a dozen hints—she'd done all those things. And he'd resisted, as he'd planned.

Trouble was, some sort of inner itch took over an hour after he'd left Tessa's porch. It persisted through dinner, through an evening's attempt to read a book, and half the night. Sure, it would be awkward to go with Tessa, but that didn't mean he couldn't go. Spiritual niggling about how long it had been since he'd been back to a church service aside, logical reasons to go kept coming to him. Quietly slipping into a back pew could give him a chance to view the townspeople, to get a stronger feel for Wander Canyon. He could observe the congregation before meeting them at the barbecue—because he knew there was no way Tessa would let him wiggle out of that invitation. Attending a service would allow him to see and hear Pastor Newton, too. He might need a dose of spiritual guidance before this was all over.

Neal had carefully timed his entrance to a few minutes after the service started. That way no one would have a chance to attempt the high-voltage welcome some churches were famous for. If he liked what he saw, he'd make a few connections after the service, but he wanted the chance to observe unseen.

He chose an unoccupied pew and settled in on the outer edge by the sanctuary's pretty stained-glass windows just as the choir was finishing their opening hymn. Minneapolis had its share of large fancy congregations and small local ones, and he'd always preferred the latter— back when he'd gone to church regularly. Some things were the same everywhere— slightly battered hymnbooks, choirs with one gifted soloist backed up by a host of singers with perhaps more heart than talent, a homey mix of announcements covering everything from Bible studies to potlucks to youth groups and preschool activities.

Neal had expected to feel uncomfortable, but was surprised that he didn't. When an older gentleman turned and smiled at him, Neal found himself smiling back. He scanned the congregants until he found Norma Binton, up front in the very first pew. She sat alone, and that stuck with him in ways he wasn't ready to accept. She struck him as the kind of woman who'd made choices that had let her end up alone. Where was the grace in that kind of judgment? *You're biased,* he told himself. *This will only work if you come at it with an open mind. Well, more open than what you've got now.*

He'd half expected to make a quick exit after the service was over, but chose instead to linger just a bit.

"Don Redding," said the older man in front of him who had offered the earlier smile. "Fellow latecomer. Some days it takes these old bones a while to get a move on in the morning."

Neal shook his hand. "Neal Rodgers. Just plain late."

"Welcome just the same. New in town?"

"Just here for a few weeks on vacation." That was such a gross understatement, it almost felt like a lie.

"Oh, you picked a pretty time to come

to the canyon. July is my favorite time of year."

A pregnant woman walked up to Don and gave him a peck on the cheek. "Hi, Dad."

"My daughter, Toni," Don explained. "And this is her husband, Bo. I'm about to become a grandfather." Don's pride at that last fact was impossible to miss.

"Congratulations to all of you," Neal replied.

"This is Neal. In town for a few weeks on vacation."

Bo pointed at Neal. "Hey, you're the runner, aren't you? My partner Jake said he and his boy met you the other day at The Depot. Bought you your first carousel ride."

"Everyone's gotta have a ride," Don agreed.

"How are you liking Wander Canyon so far?" Toni asked.

Now, there was a complicated question. Neal was scrambling for a safe way to answer when Tessa came rushing up. "Neal!"

"I see you've met Tessa," Toni said.

"He's staying at the house next to mine. I invited him to come to church with me, but evidently he sneaked in on his own."

"Yeah," Neal admitted. "Last-minute decision." A trio of happily chatting older ladies walked past them in the aisle, stopping to make a fuss over Toni's pregnant belly. Tessa laughed with them, thankfully drawing the conversation elsewhere for a moment. Out of the corner of his eye, Neal saw Norma making her way down the outer aisle. No one was stopping and saying hello to her.

His pulse jumped as he realized her gaze was leveled in his direction. Intently, and not exactly kindly. Did she recognize him from that one meeting in the drugstore? He wasn't ready for her to recognize him.

Norma stopped, however, half a dozen pews in front of him, to talk to a young family gathering their things to leave.

"You really ought to teach that child to behave in church," she said sharply. "You can never know what lost soul you're distracting from worship with all that noise."

Neal couldn't remember being distracted by the young child's behavior, but nonetheless, he felt as if Norma's comment about a lost soul was directed at him.

"Oh, Norma," one of the older ladies chided with a wagging finger at Norma, "stop that. Children are a blessing. Crying babies are a part of life." She returned her gaze to Toni. "Don't you mind Norma. When that beautiful baby is born, you bring him or her right into church and don't mind the noise one bit. Because we won't, either."

"Not one bit," a second sweet-faced grandmotherly type chimed in. "We may even ask to hold the little one. I've been spit up on by some of Wander Canyon's crankiest babies, and I consider it a badge of honor."

They all laughed. Neal was once again

struck by the vision of what life might have been like to have been raised in this community. The clash of Norma's cold nature with the warmth of this town hounded him with a wave of what-ifs.

As the group moved toward the church fellowship hall for the traditional post-service coffee hour, Neal didn't resist going along.

At least, not until Tessa tugged his elbow and pulled him aside in the hallway. "See that?" she whispered with an excited grin. "Wander's filled with sweet women old enough to be your mother. It'll be amazing when you finally meet her. Everyone will be happy for you."

Of course, no one would assume his mother was Norma Binton. No one would ever think of Old Biddy Binton in that way.

So what would they think of him when they found out? If they ever found out? Norma hadn't stayed for coffee, and no one seemed to miss her in the slightest.

This welcoming community barely tolerated the mean old woman who had given him life.

He'd come to find out who his mother was and what she was like. He was learning that this woman would add little to his life. Certainly not in light of the loving and nurturing woman—much like the happy grandmothers he'd just met—who'd been a mother to him.

Maybe the biggest message he'd take away from this church service was that some secrets simply ought to stay secrets.

"Mom, Dad, this is Neal. He's staying in the house next door. He's the one who helped me with the kittens."

"Hello there." Dad offered a friendly hand to Neal while Mom didn't exactly hide her sizing up of the new neighbor. Tessa hoped Neal didn't pick up on Mom's quick, raised-eyebrow sideways glance. To her, it nearly shouted *You didn't mention he was this handsome.*

"Has Tessa pawned a kitten off on you yet?" Mom asked sweetly.

"I've managed to resist," Neal said graciously enough that Tessa was grateful he hadn't picked up on Mom's unspoken vibe.

"Well," offered Dad, "she did say you were a vet, so I doubt you need another animal in your life."

"Vet on vacation," Neal added. Tessa hadn't thought he'd minded all the help he'd given her. She actually felt as if they were becoming friends. His quick correction gave her a twinge of guilt. *You always go too far.* She'd never considered offering one of the kittens to Neal, and now she was glad it hadn't occurred to her.

Tessa tried to shift the conversation. "Neal's from Minneapolis."

"Big-city guy, huh?" Dad replied. "Our little church must be a change for you."

Neal shrugged. "In a nice way." Tessa remembered his "not enough" reply when she'd asked him if he did attend church.

"Did you invite Neal to the barbecue Wednesday?" Mom wasn't earning points for subtlety this morning.

Tessa caught Neal's eye in a split-second *I'm sorry* glance. Since he'd changed his mind and chosen to come to service, she wanted the man to feel welcome, not pounced upon.

"She did. I'm looking forward to it."

"Best eating there is. Pastor and his crew grill a mean set of ribs, and you can't beat all the fixings the locals set out. Everybody comes." Dad elbowed Neal's arm. "Even out-of-towners."

"Speaking of which, I need to go talk to Pauline Walker about the table decorations." Mom added, "Come on, Ben. Let's leave these two alone." With that, she tugged on Dad's arm and bustled off to the other side of the parlor with a knowing look that made Tessa cringe.

"Mothers," she muttered as soon as Mom was out of earshot. Then she remembered that might not be the most sensitive thing to say around a man in Neal's situation. "Oops, sorry."

She was grateful Neal managed an awkward chuckle. "No, it's okay. I have a mom. And she's wonderful. But like yours, she can get a bit…"

"Pushy?" Tessa cut in. "Really, I'm sorry. She's been on a tear lately about my single status. I didn't mean for you to get caught in the cross fire."

"I've gotten my share of those blatant nudges from my mom, too." Neal picked up another cookie from the table spread with coffee urns and cookie trays along one side of the room. "She thinks all my current…unrest is because I'm not dating enough."

Tessa looked at him. "Your parents really don't know you're looking for—" she remembered to lower her voice "—*her*?"

"I haven't found the right way to tell them. It feels… I don't know…ungrateful. Like saying they haven't given me everything I needed when they really have."

Tessa watched his eyes scan the room. She voiced the thought she'd had over and over this morning. "She could be here. In this room."

It was the wrong thing to say. Neal's expression closed up right in front of her. "Don't. Please."

Tessa wanted to clamp her hand over her mouth. "I'm sorry. I don't want to make you regret telling me anything. Rampant curiosity is great in reporters, but maybe not always in friends."

She watched his face for a reaction to her use of the word *friends*. His features were still closed up, as if he were casting his thoughts far away. "I hope I'm your friend, not just some annoying neighbor," she went on. It seemed like the more she said, the worse she dug herself in. "If you need to go..."

He set the coffee cup down, and regret tightened Tessa's chest. "Yeah, I should."

She didn't want to let things end on this note. "Neal," she ventured, touching his elbow as he turned to go. His eyes glanced down at the contact before he looked back to her. Tessa wished she could read those eyes, figure out what he was thinking and how not to stumble over his situation. "I'm glad you came today," she offered. "I hope you got a little of something you needed."

"I did, thanks," he said. But somehow Tessa couldn't be sure Neal was talking about the church service.

She stared after him as he walked toward the church door, his sunken shoulders framed in the bright Colorado sunlight. She didn't know what to do about the strong pull she felt toward him. She loved to help people. She was always eager and happy to use her skills when folks came to her. She'd helped Mari when she'd first come back to town with her daughters. She'd helped Molly Bradshaw uncover— and eventually heal—her husband's dark past. With Neal, her help seemed to come with such high consequences. She always seemed to say the wrong thing. And yet...

well, Mom wasn't picking up on the chemistry out of nowhere. When Neal let his guard down—which wasn't often—she saw something in his eyes. Something that mirrored the gentle but insistent hum in her own heart. Still...

"Tessa," came a voice behind her. "Tessa?"

She turned to find Pastor Newton holding a stack of ancient-looking books.

He smiled. "You were a million miles away just then. Someplace good, I hope?"

"I don't know yet," she replied. *Isn't that the truth?*

"I dug up all those baptism records you asked me for. You may regret it. This stuff looks old and dusty and tedious." He brushed a cobweb off the spine of the bottom book as if to make his point.

She took the stack of books from him. "Oh, no. This is a treasure. Sure, you have to go digging, but there's always something in there. Are you sure I can keep them for a while?"

Pastor Newton laughed. "I don't think

we'll have an urgent need for the last ninety years of baptism records. And we know where to find you if we do. What are you looking for, by the way?"

Tessa ran her hand over one of the ledgers. "I don't know yet. I expect it'll jump out at me when I see it. That's usually how it works."

"Wander Canyon needs its history written down. We've got loads of it. Some of it's bound to be pretty entertaining. Sign me up for the first copy when it's ready, will you?"

"Sure thing." The way this week had gone, Tessa wondered how long it would be before this project came anywhere near completion. Still, she was grateful for Pastor Newton's support. It felt good that so many people were eager to trust her with a project like this. *See, you do help. Remember that.*

"Dawn said that was your new neighbor in town for an extended vacation."

So Mom was chatting up Neal to Pastor

Newton as well? Tessa felt her jaw clench, and tried to remember that Neal would be off Mom's newly sharpened radar within a matter of weeks. "Yes, that's Neal Rodgers."

"He had kind of a lost-soul look to him just now. Everything okay?" Pastor Newton had a reverend's radar of his own. One of the things she liked most about the man was his canny ability to sense when someone needed counsel or support. "God's nudges," he always called them, and they were almost always right.

"He seems to be sorting through some things, yes." It certainly wasn't her place to say any more than that. "Nice guy, though."

"Your mother seems to think so." Pastor Newton's smile held just a touch of commiseration.

Tessa fought the urge to roll her eyes. "Tell me about it."

Pastor Newton laughed. "I won't go all pastoral on him, I promise. But if I see him in The Depot or around town in the next week, maybe I'll try and strike up a conversation. He did come to service today. That always tells me something." He nodded at the stack of books. "Well, let me know what pops up out of all those. If there is treasure in all that history, I can't wait to hear about it."

History—it could be as much of a curse as a treasure, couldn't it? Tessa thought about all Neal was struggling with, all he might be about to discover. And Neal's mother—whoever she was—her life couldn't help but be dramatically altered by their meeting as well. That sounded like a place where God ought to be showing up in all kinds of ways.

Chapter Eight

Wednesday evening, Tessa met Neal at the top of their shared driveway to walk down to the barbecue.

"What's in there?" he asked with a playful curiosity, moving to lift the lid of the picnic basket she held.

Tessa slapped her hand onto the lid, keeping it closed. "Only the world's most delicious corn muffins."

"Can I carry that for you?"

It wasn't that heavy, but Tessa was still charmed by his gentlemanly offer to carry it. "Only if you promise not to snack on the way."

Neal grinned as Tessa allowed him to take the basket from her arms. "Afraid I'll ruin my appetite?"

There was a nervous warmth to their conversation. A not-quite-flirting tone Tessa didn't know how to classify. He was a caring man. She wasn't quite ready to believe that caring was personal to her, even if she did think she might like the idea. Still, she didn't want them to be seen as a "couple." Not with this town's wagging tongues on the lookout.

Don't think of him as anything other than a good friend making sure you didn't show up to this event alone.

Tessa kept the conversation bright and easy. "Wait till you see the food at this thing. You had better bring all the appetite you've got. If there's anything Wander Canyon folks know how to do well, it's eat."

They walked on for a few minutes before Neal asked, "Is it okay to ask if you talked to Greg today?" She was touched that he'd remembered that this was Greg's fifteenth birthday, and his first away from her. It was half the reason she'd decided to come, even though she was worried all the happy families would make her lonesome for her boy.

"I called him this morning," she replied, glad to find confidence in her voice. "I didn't want to spend the day pouting about him calling me, and it is his birthday, after all."

"And?"

"I actually got a pleasant conversation out of him. Details, some random thoughts, and a ratting out of Nick's terrible housekeeping. I have to admit I found that last one amusing. Especially considering the usual state of Greg's room. Sometimes I have to remind myself what color the carpet in his bedroom is because I go weeks without seeing it."

Neal laughed.

He was so often dark and thoughtful that it stood out like starlight when he laughed.

She shot up a quick prayer. *Let him have a good time tonight, Lord. I don't want him to regret coming with me.*

Tessa saved the best for last. "I even got an 'I miss you, Mom.' What do you think about that?"

Neal shifted the basket to his other arm. "I think that boy realized how badly he botched your last conversation."

"Could be. I'll take it, either way. Do you realize what kind of gold an unsolicited 'I miss you, Mom' is in the parenting world?"

Neal stiffened just a bit, taking some of the ease from the air between them. Tessa instantly regretted the brag. Every comment about mothers and sons was loaded with baggage for him.

"I'll make you a deal," she said, venturing a small touch to his elbow. He'd worn a blue chambray shirt that did amazing things to his brown eyes, and she enjoyed walking down the street with a man as handsome as he was.

"What kind of deal?"

"I think we're both going to have a nice time tonight. But I also think there's a pretty good chance it might start to feel like too much for either one of us. So let's set a signal to let the other know they're done."

He turned to her. "I'd go whenever you were ready."

"Thank you, but I wanted you to know I'd do the same for you as well."

His brows furrowed—half serious, half in play. "I'm a big boy. I can walk myself home from the church barbecue."

"So can I," she countered. "But this isn't about safety. Well, not the physical kind. There's a lot going on for both of us. I like knowing I have an escape hatch if I need it."

Neal shook his head. "Do you mother everyone like this, or just me?"

How could she answer that? She did feel a strong urge to protect him, to help him sort through the challenge of connecting with his birth mother. But it was also so nice not to have to do something alone for a change. She ignored his question and continued presenting her plan. "Our code word will be *pretzels*."

That brought a laugh from him. "*Pretzels?* You just got done telling me the place will be loaded down with every kind of food and you chose *pretzels*?"

Tessa stopped walking. "Do you have a better idea? A word that won't sound completely random and out of context when we say it?"

"Well, I suppose you have a point there. *Pretzels*, it is." But he shook his head again as he agreed to the strategy.

"Most days I can do the happy family thing on my own. Greg and I are a family, after all. And I'm glad all my friends have found happiness. Really, I am. It's just hard to be the odd one out at some of these things. Don't you ever feel like that?" Tessa realized she'd never asked him about his current relationships. "Or is there someone waiting for you back in Minneapolis?"

"Let's just say I might give Greg a run for his money in the 'botch it' department." Neal paused before adding, "I don't think I feel complete enough lately to be in a relationship. Does that make any sense?"

Tessa let herself hold his gaze for a bit longer than was a good idea. "Total sense." They turned the final corner and the church front lawn came into view. Despite how awkward it felt, Tessa took the basket back from him, not wanting to give anyone any ideas.

The Wander Canyon Community Church Annual Barbecue was in full swing. Delectable scents filled the air as the sun began to go down behind the trees that lined the church lawn. The place was strewn with so many lights that it glowed like Main Street at Christmas. Happy chatter filled the air as guests wandered among the many picnic tables laden with brightly colored cloths, table settings, and buffet tables that had enough food to feed a town three times this size.

"It's like something out of a movie," Neal said with a touch of disbelief as they walked up. "I didn't realize stuff like this still happened."

"Every summer. Even Greg managed to admit he was sorry to miss this."

Neal looked around. "Is everyone in town here?"

Tessa wondered if there was a second, unspoken question behind that one. *Is she here?* Nearly everyone in town was here, and so she voiced the answer to both questions. "Most likely, yes."

Neal swallowed hard.

"You okay?" This night was somewhat hard for her, but it was a whopping brand of hard for him.

"Yeah," he said a bit unsteadily. "I think so."

"Remember, there are always *pretzels*."

* * *

Tessa seemed to know everyone. And she didn't hesitate to introduce Neal to everybody she knew. Was that just who she was, or was Tessa methodically taking him through the entire older female population of Wander Canyon on purpose?

It would happen eventually, the way she was going. She would introduce him to Norma Binton. And while he was enjoying himself now, Neal couldn't say if that would send him running for *pretzels*. But, of course, he couldn't use the code word right away, or it would be a clear signal to Tessa which Wander Canyon woman was his birth mother.

"Any chance we can eat now?" he'd asked when the parade of neighbors became a bit too much. "I skipped lunch to save room for all this."

Tessa laughed. "You sound too much like Greg."

"You okay?" Neal would be lying if

he said he didn't like the way she smiled softly at his inquiry.

"I'm doing fine. Helps to have you here." She blushed a bit at the admission, but he'd been thinking the very same thing.

"Thanks for dragging me with you."

She laughed again at his choice of wording, and they each took one of the extra-large paper plates stacked at the head of the buffet table.

While the assortment of food was as enormous as she'd said, Neal's favorite offering was the bowl of pretzels. They'd caught each other's eye as they both skipped it.

They settled themselves at one of the many picnic tables, and Neal made sure to sit opposite Tessa rather than next to her. It was the smart thing to do so no one would get any ideas, but he felt a bit of regret at not being close to her. She had a way of bolstering him, making him feel comfortable. It was a welcome change from the fish-out-of-water-on-a-life-changing-mission sensation that usually surrounded him.

A little boy bounded up to her. "Mom says you have kittens."

"Hey, sport. Yes, I do. Quite a few, in fact."

A couple walking hand in hand came up behind the boy. Neal recognized the woman from the coffee shop—and as the talented soloist from the church service. "Zack, we told you to wait until we had our food before asking."

"Hi, Molly. Hello, Sawyer." Tessa's eyes brightened as she turned to the boy. "A kitten, huh?"

"I'm thinking about it," Zack said with a seriousness beyond his years. "But I got a lot of questions."

Tessa patted the bench next to her for the boy to sit down. "I'll answer as many of them as I can, and maybe Dr. Neal here can answer some, too. He's a veterinarian."

"Pop-Tarts is a vet?" Molly said as she sat.

Neal immediately regretted ever mentioning to Molly that he usually ate Pop-Tarts for breakfast. She'd called him Pop-Tarts multiple times since. People knew everything about each other in a small town like this. Well, almost everything. He was living proof that even Wander Canyon held its secrets.

Tessa gave a *you kidding me?* look in Neal's direction, but Zack seemed to find this enormously impressive. "Mom never lets me have those." Neal couldn't decide if he'd just made a new friend in Zack or a new enemy in his mother.

"Not *every* morning," Neal felt compelled to declare. "So you're thinking about a kitten, are you?" he said more to save himself than to launch a session of professional advice.

"Yep," Zack said. "But I need to be sure."

He'd dealt with enough impulse-purchase kittens and puppies to admire Zack's thoughtfulness. "Are you ready to take care of it? Even when it isn't fun or you don't feel like it?"

"We've talked it through," said the man who sat next to Neal. "Sawyer," he introduced himself as he offered a handshake.

"Nice to meet all of you." Neal found himself meaning it. The little town and its friendly residents were growing on him.

"*Dr. Rodgers*—" Molly made a show of emphasizing his real name "—is here on vacation, so we can't bother him with too many questions."

Zack reached into his jacket pocket and pulled out a stack of index cards at least an inch high bound by three different rubber bands. "But I have lots."

"How about we pick just five for now?" Molly gave Neal an apologetic look.

"Five for Miss Tessa and five for Dr. Rodgers?" Zack asked.

"Five altogether," Sawyer said. "You can ask them while we grab our food, okay?"

Zack looked at his mother. "Only get stuff I like."

"Just the usual, I promise," replied Molly. "Okay with you two?" She bounced a friendly look between Neal and Tessa.

"Just fine," Tessa said. She leaned into Zack as soon as Molly and Sawyer were gone. "Ask as many as you want until they get back. We don't mind."

To his amazement, Neal found he didn't mind, either.

Zack directed his first question to Tessa. "Are they cute?"

"Totally adorable," Tessa gushed. "Greg is excited we get to keep Charlie for ourselves."

Greg had, in fact, been thrilled to know he was coming home to a new pet. Tessa had played it up so much that Neal wondered if she wasn't using little Charlie as an extra incentive to ensure Greg returned in time to start high school.

Zack looked up at Neal for his next question. "Do they get sick? Do they die?"

Neal considered carefully before answering. "Yes, cats and kittens do get sick every once in a while. All animals do. But veterinarians help with that." He looked the boy directly in the eyes. "You've gotten sick, right?"

"I had the flu last year. And Mom got really sick once." Tessa caught Neal's eye as if to hint that there was a story behind that answer.

"And you're both better now, right?"

"Uh-huh." Zack nodded.

"It's the same with cats. Most of the time, they're healthy and lots of fun. So if you promise to take care of them, you'll do great."

"But do they die?" Zack persisted.

Just how thick was that stack of question cards? "Most times not for a long, long time. I had a cat when I was your age. His name was Tiger, and he lived for fourteen long years. I was sad when he finally died, but I was much happier for all the time we had together."

Zack considered this information for a moment, then moved this card to the bottom of the stack as well. Neal exhaled, glad to have given an answer the boy seemed to find satisfactory.

"Do you have one with stripes?" he asked Tessa.

"Blake, Kenny and Patsy all have stripes," she replied. "Of course, that's only the names I gave them. You can pick out your own name for the one you choose."

"I want a boy cat," Zack said. "I hafta think about the name part." After another sorting of the cards, he asked Neal, "Can he sleep with me?"

Finally, one slightly easier to answer. "They like to, but it depends on what you want. And your mom and dad. Tiger slept with me for part of the night, but other parts I think he liked to wander around the house." On impulse, Neal added, "But Tiger always seemed to know when I needed him. If I was sad or sick or lonely, he was always right there. And he loved to play with me, too."

Zack went through four more questions

before Molly and Sawyer returned with three plates heaping with food.

"How about we let Miss Tessa and Dr. Neal visit the dessert table while we dig in?" Molly said with a knowing look.

"And thank them for their answers," Sawyer added.

"Thanks," Zack said, wrapping his cards back up in the rubber bands.

Neal surprised himself by replying, "Anytime. And if you have more, you can find me in the house next to Miss Tessa's."

"That was really sweet," Tessa said as they made their way to the table that was piled high with all sorts of desserts. "You were great with him back there."

Great with kids wasn't how Neal would have described himself. He just nodded in reply.

"No, really. Zack's a sweet little guy, but he's a champion worrier. You were wonderful with him."

Wonderful seemed a bit of an overstatement, but Neal liked how Tessa's compliment settled in his chest.

Tessa nudged his elbow. "And Pop-Tarts? Really? You think you know a guy when he lives next to you—"

"Hello, Tessa!" Two older couples interrupted her with big hugs and bigger smiles. "Can you remember a year when we had better weather for the barbecue?"

And other neighborly chatter filled the next few minutes. "And who's your friend here?" said one of the women.

Tessa introduced Neal as her neighbor renting the house for a few weeks' vacation, nothing more. It happened two more times before they ever made it to the dessert table.

"I'll know three-quarters of the town by the time the night's over," he said.

Tessa gave a satisfied smile. "That's the idea. You'll meet everyone. Even *her*, I hope." When Neal felt his spine stiffen at the thought of a conversation with prickly Norma Binton after all the warmhearted people he'd met already, Tessa stilled. "Unless you're suddenly hungry for *pretzels* instead of dessert."

"Are you kidding?" he replied, liking the foreign feeling of a wide smile on his face. "Just look at those desserts. What fool would settle for Pop-Tarts when you can have all these?"

Chapter Nine

The dessert table was a great idea…until Neal realized there was a group of older women dishing out the sweets. One of them he'd met earlier in the evening; two were new faces. Neal's stomach dropped to his shoes when, just as he was walking up to the table with Tessa, one of the women ducked away and Norma Binton took her place.

It felt impossible to have this casual interaction and not somehow give away to someone as perceptive as Tessa that Norma was his birth mother.

Just get through it. Stick to the desserts she's not handing out.

That seemed like the safest strategy, until Tessa handed him a plate and said, "The thing here is to get a little bit of everything. Right, Dinah?"

Dinah, a plump little woman with a cheerful smile, replied, "That's what I always do." Dinah practically winked at Neal. "Best you take her advice, young man."

He was glad he could hide his nerves under the cover of Dinah's suggestion. "There must be eight desserts here." He put a hand to his stomach. He should have skipped eating for the past two days, not just lunch.

"Nine," said the woman next to Dinah, proudly. "And I wouldn't miss a one of 'em, if I were you."

Tessa held out her plate to Dinah. "Load 'er up, Dinah. A little bit of everything." She turned to Neal as Dinah was dishing out a small slice of each of the three desserts in front of her. "Dinah's apple crumble is the stuff of legend around here. I keep pestering her for the recipe, but she won't budge."

"I need to give you all some reason to keep me around," Dinah teased, reaching her hand out for Neal's plate.

He could only comply. "Looks delicious," he said. Tessa was chatting away with the next woman in line—Norma—but Neal's brain was blanking out like a floodlight at the prospect of holding an ordinary conversation with his birth mother.

"Have you met Norma Binton yet?" Tessa asked, as if it were the most normal thing in the world. He supposed it was. To her. It absolutely was *not* to him.

"I don't think so," Neal said, hoping he sounded somewhat close to casual despite the words feeling as if they squeaked out of his throat. *I'm talking to my birth mother. My mother is dishing desserts out to me and has no idea.* It was enough to make him dizzy.

Norma narrowed her eyes at him and asked, "Are you new in town?"

Every cell in his body felt as if it was going haywire. "Here on vacation." Neal was sure he was sounding like an idiot. The bowl of pretzels called to him from the food table, urging him to say the word and walk away from all this.

"Neal is staying at Valerie's rental house next to me," Tessa explained. Thankfully, she seemed to have no idea of the gravity of the moment for him. "I told him he couldn't miss the barbecue tonight."

"No, sirree," chimed in Dinah. "Can't miss this."

"Bit of everything, then?" Norma's face was so exasperatingly neutral, Neal couldn't tell if she approved of the idea. It felt ridiculous to care.

"Tessa says it's the thing to do," he managed to blurt out.

"Welcome to Wander Canyon," said the third woman. He remembered her from the ticket booth at the carousel. She held her hand out for his plate. "Didn't I see you in service on Sunday?"

Relief spread through Neal's chest. He'd made it through this challenge—or so he hoped. "Yes. It's a nice church you've got there."

"Well, I always say our faith is only exceeded by our appetite." She held a spoon over a large bowl of white fluff. "Want some whipped cream on that cherry pie? I make it up from scratch—none of that canned nonsense."

"Sure." And with that, he'd finished his tour of the dessert table. *No big deal*, he declared to himself.

Neal did his best to keep up his end of the conversation as they walked back to their table with the overflowing plates. "I'm going to need to double my morning run," he even managed to joke.

"Oh, it's just one meal," Tessa replied, gently swatting his arm. "And you look like you're in pretty good shape to me."

It had been so long since Neal noticed a

woman paying attention to him that it was a good ten seconds before he realized she might be flirting with him. The fact that the prospect appealed to him was almost as shocking as his trip to the dessert table. "Not if I keep eating meals like this."

Tessa helped herself to a spoonful of apple cobbler. "This from a man who eats Pop-Tarts for breakfast. You're going to have a hard time living that down, by the way."

Neal laughed at the sparkle in her eyes. He'd done it. He'd talked to Norma Binton as if she were just an ordinary person and the world hadn't caved in around him. He owed Tessa for that—or that was how it felt. She'd made the night ordinary—extraordinary, in fact—for him, and he was grateful.

The gratitude simmered into something a little warmer as he reached out and thumbed a dollop of whipped cream off her chin. The moment was like the whole evening itself—perfectly ordinary and then not at all ordinary. Her eyes told him she felt the contact as much as he did, sending off little warning signals he was sorely tempted to ignore.

"Everyone's so nice here," he said. It sounded goofy, but he was still scrambling for his bearings.

"You were expecting something different?" Her voice held a touch of seriousness. She recognized the power of his visit here, the lifelong impact of what he'd come to do.

"I don't know what I was expecting," he admitted. That wasn't exactly true. He'd expected to meet someone a whole lot nicer, a whole lot more admirable than who Norma had turned out to be. "I guess I was expecting to eat less," he joked to cover the moment.

Tessa dug into Pauline's cherry pie. "Wrong town for that."

Tessa kept casting glances up at the stars as she and Neal walked home from the barbecue. The sky drew her gaze half because of the exquisite sapphire blue of the summer sky tonight, and half because she needed someplace other to look than at Neal. The pull she was feeling toward him was growing too fast for her comfort. And yet things were startlingly comfortable between them.

She knew he was deep in thought. Tessa was nearly certain that Neal's birth mother had been somewhere in the crowd of people tonight. She'd tried not to analyze his every reaction, looking for clues in even the most casual of conversations. It felt like prying to try to guess who "she" was, but her reporter's curiosity refused to be tamped down. He knew. And he knew she didn't—or could only guess. It made for a strange but enticing electricity between them.

Still, there was more than just Neal's parental search. Tessa could sense that he was as aware of her beside him as she was of his presence. The evening had been both wonderful and difficult—the hours had flown by in layers of emotions both lovely and prickly. As comfortable as she was with the silence between them, the quiet seemed to roar with a flurry of feelings. A heightened sense of awareness. A careful, just-emerging glow of attraction.

Tessa felt her skin heat up as she recalled the moment he'd touched her chin to wipe off the whipped cream. She was glad she had been sitting—she likely would have swayed into his touch. The man really did have the most amazing hands.

She found herself hyperaware of how close or far her hand was to his. Tessa told herself to abandon the ridiculous hope that he might slip his hand around hers as they walked home. It would be warm and strong. It would feel so good to walk under tonight's spectacular sky hand in hand with a man as handsome and tender as Neal Rodgers.

A man with a mountain of issues, she reminded herself, and who was heading back to Minneapolis in two weeks. That should have squelched the empty feeling in her palm, but it didn't.

She decided to break the silence. "I'll never ask, you know."

He stopped walking and looked at her. Tessa could watch him drag his thoughts back to the current moment. Did he know his thoughts showed so plainly on his face? After the baffling hormonal tornado that was Greg, Tessa's tender clarity with Neal felt amazing. Invigorating. Downright enticing, when she was honest.

"Ask what?" His expression told her the question was unnecessary. He knew exactly what she was talking about.

"I'll never ask you who she is."

His eyebrows rose. "Don't you want to know?"

"Of course I want to know. I'm *dying* to know. I've been making guesses all night. But..." Her words fell off, not sure how to explain what she wanted him to know.

"But what?"

"It's your secret. And I won't ever press you to tell me. I hope you'll maybe feel like you can tell me. Before you leave, that is. I hope you feel like everyone can know, that it'll be an amazing happy reunion and you'll get the kind of ending you were hoping for." She felt bold enough to add, "I want that for you. For her, too, now that I think about it."

Neal seemed stunned by her declaration. He squinted his eyes shut for a moment and she watched his jaw tighten.

"What?" she questioned, fighting the urge to put her hand on his arm. "Don't you think that can happen?" There was something huge lurking under all this, something she didn't yet know. Something she had no right to know if Neal chose never to share it. For someone who'd been trained to unearth facts people might not be ready to share, the urge to treat this particular fact with extreme care hummed in her chest.

"Seems a bit much to hope for," he said.

The resignation in his voice pierced her. Everyone had been so welcoming to him tonight. Even Norma Binton had been something close to civil, and that almost never happened. He had to feel good about every woman he'd met tonight. And yet his eyes held none of the optimism she felt.

"How could any mom not be proud of the person you've become?" she asked more to herself than to Neal as they turned up the shared driveway. "How could any woman not be pleased to know you've grown up into such a fine man? The way you talked with Zack? Seriously, I thought Molly was going to offer you free coffee for life."

When he didn't reply, she stopped. His eyes were on the ground, his shoulders a bit slumped.

"Neal," she said, touching his elbow. He looked up at her, and she knew for certain he felt every bit of the hum between them that she did. "What are you afraid of?"

His response was to sit on her porch steps. Tessa sat next to him. She'd wait out his wrestling, bear witness to whatever it was that kept him from taking this next important step. What was the point of coming all this way if not to reveal himself to the woman who'd given him life?

"You tell yourself fairy tales when you're adopted," he said softly. "You make up glorious, noble things about who your parents are and why they gave you up. And then you discover they're just human beings who made mistakes and ended up in situations they wouldn't choose. I mean, no one gives up a child because they *want* to, right? Maybe it's better not to know the details. Maybe the stories are a better thing to hang on to than the hard facts of what really happened."

That seemed such a sad way to look at it. "And maybe there's an amazing story here. Maybe you get to fill the hole that's been gaping all this time. You must want to know, need to know. You wouldn't be here if you didn't."

Neal looked at her as if she were a cock-eyed optimist looking for a happy ending that wasn't there. She was. Some deep inner instinct—the Holy Spirit, she hoped—told her there was a good ending to Neal's quest, if he'd just be brave enough to reach for it.

He had to reach for it. It wouldn't be handed to him, and she certainly couldn't reach in his place. They sat for a long while, feeling the significance of the stars seep into their souls the way only a Colorado evening could. A shooting star even soared across the sky as they sat. "Make a wish," she said instinctively, the way every parent did when children saw falling stars.

Neal turned to her. For a breathless moment, she thought he was going to kiss her. That would have been her wish, had she not given the wish to him. She would have liked for him to kiss her. Despite all the reasons why there was no future for her with him, she would have gladly taken this moment as the gift that it was.

He did not kiss her. He did not touch her or take her hand in his. He looked at her for the longest moment, took a deep breath and said, "I will tell you." Tessa swallowed hard. She knew what a monumental thing that was for him to say. "Just not...tonight."

"Tell *her*," she pleaded, as much for the unknown mother's sake as for the tumult consuming the man in front of her. "Don't leave without telling her. I'm going to make you pinkie-promise," she tried to joke. But the moment was too serious and it fell flat. "You've got to," she insisted, knowing it was true even though she couldn't say how she knew.

A little bit of the lightness returned to his eyes. "Are you always this pushy?"

"Only when it really matters. And this time it really matters."

Chapter Ten

Tessa sat curled up in one of the plush chairs in her study. It was the wee hours of Thursday morning, and she'd been half poring over the books Pastor Newton had given her and half being entertained by kitten antics. "Since none of us can sleep—" she addressed the litter, charmingly playful despite it being the middle of the night "—we might as well do something useful."

She wasn't doing a very good job of keeping her eyes from wandering in the direction of Neal's kitchen window. The lights were still on.

"I pinkie-promised myself," she declared to the sets of yellow eyes that watched her. "No visits, no texts, no calls. No more contact tonight. Even though, technically, it *is* tomorrow." Her clock had chimed 1:00 a.m. half an hour ago. *Nope. No. Don't.*

The kittens began burrowing themselves into a towel for amusement, and Dolly took advantage of the free moment. She leaped up onto the chair and promptly planted herself down right in the middle of Tessa's book.

"Oh, please," Tessa cajoled, "don't let me keep you. It's not like I was reading or anything." She tried to scoot Dolly off the old book without success. "Actually, I wasn't really reading, was I?"

Dolly replied by settling further and emitting a loud, happy purr.

"Tell you what. I'll give you a moment's peace if you do the same for me." Tessa gently tugged the text out from under Dolly to balance it on the chair's thick upholstered arm. She worked a finger down the long page of baptismal records, squinting at the faded handwriting on the yellowed page. The names were listed in date order, not alphabetical, so she had to scan every page of the likely years her ancestor Jeremiah Concord was born. The first two years' ledgers had come up empty, and Tessa was hoping this one would reveal her ancestor's baptismal record.

Three pages later, Tessa's efforts were rewarded. A listing for Jeremiah Concord showed up.

Jeremiah Gordon Concord, born to Abagail and Malcolm Concord of Colorado Territory May 13, 1904, baptized by Robert Hudson May 18, 1904.

Tessa's finger lingered on the name of her great-grandfather, recorded in flowing script into the blanks of the baptismal record. She leaned her head back against the chair and pictured the ceremony. A squalling baby sitting in the arms of her great-great-grandparents. Homespun Sunday-best clothes, wagons and bonnets and quilts. Back in the days when Wander Canyon was just a collection of mining settlements. All those generations of Concords, basking in the history of it all. There was something so grounding in it. Family histories lent a sense of perspective and place.

Something Neal was missing. After all, his line only stretched as far as himself—until now. Maybe that was where the lost look in his eyes came from, the incompleteness that drew her so strongly to him. He was a stray of a different kind, wasn't he?

"I could help him," she told Dolly, who only squinted a dubious reply. "With just that one name, I could write him up a whole history. It's probably right here," she said as she ran a hand across the next page of entries. "He seems about my age. It wouldn't be hard at all."

Except it would. There was something Neal wasn't telling her—something more than just the name of his birth mother. As if he'd gotten to this gap in his history and was staring at it, afraid to jump to the other side.

"That part's on you," Tessa said to the glow of Neal's kitchen window. "You've got to want to leap. I'm certainly not going to push you." Two of the kittens got in a scuffle, and Dolly leaped off Tessa's lap to go tend to her youngsters. "Look at me, talking to a window," Tessa said, glad to feel a yawn stretch her words. "Okay, Jeremiah, I've found your birth." Notating the ledger and page and info in her notebook, Tessa picked up another book marked *Marriage Records*. "Let's find that pretty little lady you married."

An hour later, Tessa had filled her notebook with names, dates, volumes and page numbers. She'd worked her way up to the citations of her own father's generation. A smile warmed Tessa's face as she found the listing of her parents' marriage in 1983.

Mom and Dad. There was a cheerful photo of their wedding day in the hallway of the house where she'd grown up. She often touched the wood framing the shiny-faced bride and groom as she walked by, enjoying their smitten smiles. Theirs was a love that lasted. It had been hard not to live up to that, to watch her own marriage pale by comparison.

Oh, the dated hairstyles and clothes of Mom and Dad's wedding photo always amused her—that hair and those puffy sleeves!—but she'd known the love and optimism she saw in those newlyweds. She had wonderful parents. Good and decent people who grounded her in faith and community. And they were doing the same for Greg. Nick may have been a stumble in that road, but she'd overcome it. And maybe someday she'd be sitting in the aisle at Wander Canyon Community Church watching Greg take a bride into his life.

Tessa considered making a duplicate of the marriage record to frame it. She could have one, and perhaps give one to Mom and Dad for their anniversary. Even though she knew there were digital records in some file somewhere, there was something timeless in the handwritten entry taking its place beside all the others down the years.

Yawning again, Tessa surrendered to the fact that she'd better get some sleep. Even the light in Neal's kitchen next door had finally darkened, and it was nearly two in the morning. As she closed the ledger, Tessa noticed the dates listed on the most recent edition she hadn't opened yet.

"Well, what do you know?" she asked Dolly, now curled and asleep beside her kittens in the box. "That means I'm in there." The years listed meant this edition covered the year of her own birth in 1984. It would be nice to be able to see that entry, to touch the handwritten record of her own place on the Concord family tree. A fitting close to the circle of facts she'd uncovered tonight.

So, despite the lateness of the hour, Tessa pulled open the ledger and began thumbing through the pages until she found the records for the year she was born. Her finger quickly found the notation for February.

Theresa Catherine Concord was born to Benjamin and Dawn Concord June 24, 1984, and baptized by Dawson Porterfield July 20, 1984.

Tessa's mind thought back to the photo framed on her parents' hallway wall. Mom and Dad smiled while holding her in the white baptismal blanket that had been used on so many Concord babies over the years.

Her envisioning was interrupted by the notice of a set of small details. Something wasn't quite right about the entry. "Benjamin" had been written in a slightly different pen color than the rest of the entry. And why had nearly a month passed between her birth and her baptism? Wander Canyon usually baptized babies within weeks of their births unless there was some reason not to.

So what was the reason here? And why had Dad's name been filled in separately?

Don't be silly. You're just tired, she told herself as she slipped a piece of paper in the book to mark the page and shut it. She was seeing things that weren't there. There was a perfectly logical reason why, but she wasn't going to discover it in the middle of the night. She needed to sleep. Then she could ask her parents tomorrow. Why look for drama where there wasn't any?

Neal hadn't slept well at all last night. His brain tumbling in a hundred different directions every time he tried to lie down.

Reading didn't help, nor did watching TV, or even just sitting in a chair staring at the light coming from Tessa's study.

She was up, too. He kept reading all kinds of things into that, things he had no right to imagine. Even if there was something there—which seemed absurd because there *was* definitely something there between them—now wasn't the time. She lived here and his life was in Minneapolis. Plus, he'd seen Norma. And he had a sinking feeling a happy reunion wasn't in the works here.

He knew, on some bone-deep level, that this would be his one and only trip to Wander Canyon. He dragged himself to the kitchen and put an extra spoon of coffee in the hot water because he was too exhausted to run all the way to The Depot for stronger stuff. He'd tell Norma, because that was why he'd come all this way, but it would simply be closing the book on a long mystery. Nothing was going to come of it—except maybe a bit of pain for both of them. But then the wound would close and heal. There would be a scar, but then again, hadn't there always been?

Neal managed a smile as he pulled a box of Pop-Tarts from the cupboard. He ought to buy some eggs today, or even some of those frozen breakfast sandwiches. He wanted to be able to boast to Tessa that he was eating a better breakfast than the sugary rectangles that had been his morning meal for far too many years.

He'd just put a pair of them in the toaster when someone pounded on his door.

Tessa stood there much as she had that first morning. Hair a mess, bleary just-woke-up eyes that likely matched his own, those ridiculous pink socks, and an expression of panic.

"Charlie," she blurted out the moment he opened the door. "Something's wrong with Charlie." She didn't bother to ask if he'd come this time; she simply grabbed his hand and began pulling him toward her house.

"Wait—let me get my bag," he said, slipping out of her grasp long enough to pull his medical bag from its place in the corner. Tessa grabbed his hand again so hard he had to juggle the bag in his other hand to be able to shut his door behind him. "What's wrong?"

"I found him apart from the others this morning." Tessa kept up a stream of nervous chatter as they rushed across the driveway. "He's barely moving and making the most awful whining. I don't think he's nursing. Why isn't Dolly making sure he's nursing?"

A kitten's failure to thrive wasn't that uncommon. And it could be dangerous— even fatal—if not caught quickly and treated. Neal gave her the only assurance he could at this point. "You were smart not to wait."

Tessa dashed up her porch stairs with Neal firmly in tow—she still hadn't let go of his hand—and pushed open the door to her back room. "And here I was thinking you'd be mad that I woke you up again with a kitten emergency."

"I'd never be mad." Despite the urgency of the situation, it came out a little warmer than he'd intended. Neal wasn't ready to admit to her—or anyone—how she was getting under his skin.

One quick look told Neal that Tessa was right to be alarmed. Charlie was pushed up against the back of the box, away from his mother and littermates. The signs of dehydration—a gaunt face and skin that didn't spring back when touched—along with signs of gastrointestinal distress told Neal that Charlie had indeed stopped nursing. "His breathing seems okay," he said, wanting to give Tessa the one positive he saw. "We just have to get him back on track."

It was going to be a little more complicated than that, of course. "What time does your vet's office open again?"

Tessa seemed on the verge of tears. The

unspoken *Aren't you my vet?* sank straight into his heart.

He was going to have to do the home version of treatment—at least until he could convince Tessa to take Charlie in to Dr. Davidson. "Did Dr. Davidson have you pick up any packets of kitten formula to keep on hand?"

"He did." She rummaged through a paper bag on a nearby counter and produced three packets of exactly what they needed. *Good.*

"Have you got an eyedropper?"

Her face fell. "No."

"I think I have something we can use in here." He pushed his hand around in his case until he found a plastic bag with an assortment of syringes.

"Take one of the packets and make half a batch in a glass. Mix it really good with water that's a little bit warm. No clumps. And wash the syringe. I'll see if we can't get Dolly on board while you do that."

Tessa nodded, wiping a tear off her

cheek with one hand as she took the syringe from him and raced off to the kitchen. "It's not too late," he called after her, feeling her worry pierce his gut. "It's going to be okay."

Normally, Neal tried never to make such assurances. You never did know it was going to be okay. Right now, however, his desire to comfort Tessa overrode his common sense. He wanted Charlie to make it as much as she did, because he knew what the little kitten had come to mean to her.

And he simply wasn't ready to deal with the fallout of another mother abandoning her son.

Neal placed Charlie up against Dolly's belly and gently rubbed the kitten's back and forehead. "Come on, Dolly. We stand a better chance here if you nudge him along."

Dolly began licking Charlie, which was exactly what Neal needed her to do, but it didn't seem to motivate the little guy to latch on. Neal knew Charlie was dehydrated, but he wouldn't give in to the fear that he was too far gone to nurse. Charlie had to make it. Neal knew getting so emotionally involved wasn't smart, but he didn't seem to be able to gain any professional distance on this one.

Tessa rushed back with the formula prepared exactly as he'd asked. She'd been crying. Neal felt her desperation wrap around him as he took the glass from her and used it to fill the tiny oral syringe. He placed a drop of formula on Charlie's tongue and gently used one finger to feel the kitten's throat for the motion of a swallow.

"Please, Lord," he heard Tessa pray behind him. "Please."

Neal surprised himself by saying the same small prayer in the silence of his own heart.

The movement under his finger told Neal what he needed to know. "Charlie is swallowing. That's a good sign." He placed Charlie stomach-down on a towel on his lap. Holding the tiny head stable, Neal slid the syringe into the kitten's mouth and pushed ever so slightly on the syringe. He watched for Charlie's tongue to make the instinctive movements of swallowing, relief filling his chest as the kitten took in the first drops of formula. "There you go, little fella. Just like that. Come on back to us."

Tessa sniffled behind him and he felt one of her hands come to rest on his shoulder. "He's eating," she whispered, awe in her voice. "You got him to eat." She sniffed again and Neal felt his own throat tighten up. "Thank You, God."

There was always a deep gratification in saving an animal, especially a beloved one. He'd felt the pressure of that burden hit him hard lately, and it occurred to him that part of his weariness was due to the fact that he'd forgotten God's place in the wonder of creating and saving animals. He'd mostly forgotten God altogether. It seemed wrong that this morning was the first time in years he'd prayed over an animal in danger.

It was slow going at first, but Charlie finished enough formula to let Neal believe he'd pull through. There was more to it than just this one meal, but it was a start. After he wiped Charlie's tiny face and settled him in next to Dolly and the rest of his littermates, Neal found himself whispering to the kitten. "How about we do the next one old-school? Mama style."

Tessa managed a small laugh of huge relief. "He's going to be okay?"

Neal straightened, reminded of how tired he was and how poorly he'd slept. "For now. You should take him to the vet, but Dr. Davidson will probably tell you to do exactly what we just did if he doesn't return to nursing. If he doesn't, you'll have to bottle-feed him. That's not a small commitment."

"I'll do it," she said with no hesitation whatsoever. "I'll do whatever it takes." Tessa looked at him for a long moment, blinked away more tears and then wrapped her arms around him.

He should have backed away. He should have told her he'd only done what any vet would have done. Instead, Neal found himself helpless to do anything but return her embrace. He could feel the relief soften her shoulders, feel the soft shake of her chest and the warm wet spot as she cried a little bit onto his shirt. "I know you'll take great care of him," he said, finding it the safest thing to say of all the feelings rushing through him at the moment. For the smallest second, Neal let his chin rest on the top of her head, undone by the power of the moment. Something old and hard broke free deep in his chest, falling away before he could stop it.

"I will take good care of him," Tessa said as she pulled away. The moment had become far more intimate than either of them was ready for. She fumbled with her hair, wiping her eyes. Neal was so endeared by the gesture that he thought if he stayed another moment he might kiss her.

He was just telling himself—for the third time—to reach for his bag and go home when Tessa looked him straight in the eye and said, "I will, you know. Take the best care of him. Because that's what moms do, right? We take care when care is needed, no matter what."

As the words left her mouth, her eyes widened as she realized the power of those words to someone like Neal. Did she even realize her hand came up to cover her mouth as if to erase the bone-deep sentiment she so easily believed? One he so resented right now?

"Not always," he said, feeling as if the words burned him as he spoke. It pushed up out of him, relentless and unstoppable. A terrible counterpoint to all the hope and determination in Tessa's eyes. "Not when your mother is Norma Binton."

Chapter Eleven

Norma? Tessa stared at Neal, who looked as if he'd just fallen off a very high cliff. "It's Norma? Norma Binton is your birth mother?" She leaned against the wall, feeling a bit dizzy herself.

Neal ran a hand nervously through his hair. It was clear he hadn't planned to admit that to her right now. The moment had taken them both to places they weren't ready to go. "Yeah," he breathed, looking everywhere but at her. Right now he seemed as fragile as little Charlie. The metaphor of both trying to recover from the consequences of missing motherhood couldn't be denied. If she wanted proof that God was putting her in the path of Neal's journey, it was hard to ignore that proof now.

Norma Binton. A woman who was barely *nice*—more often just the opposite—much less nurturing and maternal. It seemed almost impossible, but that wasn't true. Biology could give anyone a child. It was *parenting* that was a choice. Tessa had known a dozen stories that told that truth, but none so stark as the man in front of her. "I'm sorry." It seemed both the right and the wrong thing to say.

"Yeah," Neal said again, still looking unmoored. "Me, too."

Tessa glanced down to see Charlie sleeping against Dolly's side, snuggled between the furry bodies of his brothers and sisters. "How about I put some coffee on? Dr. D's office doesn't open for another hour, and I think we need to talk about this."

Neal hesitated. "What's there to talk about?"

Tessa simply tugged him into the kitchen. No way was she going to let Neal sulk back to his house after dropping a bombshell like that.

"Well, for starters, it explains a lot." Tessa pulled the strongest coffee grounds she had out of the cupboard.

"Like what?" He sank into one of her kitchen chairs. The man looked equal parts terrified and relieved. What a whopper of a secret to be carrying around a place like Wander Canyon.

"Here I am all optimistic and introducing you to every older woman in town thinking any one of our great ladies could be your mom. I think I'm helping and you're dragging your feet trying to be cautious because… Well, come on—who *wouldn't* be if it was Norma?" She still struggled to get her head around the idea.

"She's…" He wiped his hand down his face, struggling for a word. "Daunting."

"That's putting it mildly," Tessa agreed.

"Wow. How? Do you know any of the details?"

"She was an unwed mother. She never divulged who the father was. That's about all I know. I'm not even a hundred percent sure she is my birth mother, but I know enough to go to her with what I know. That is, if I choose to."

His hesitation in the face of all her encouragement made sense now. She set the carafe under the coffee maker and turned on the brewing cycle. "I kind of always wondered what made her such a mean old thing. I figured there had to be something in her past to turn her so sour."

Neal gave her the most lost look. "Turns out it was me."

Tessa sat across from him. "No. No, you can't think like that. You didn't make Norma who she is. She chose to be that way. This isn't on you."

He didn't respond. He only looked at her as if he'd been waiting a very long time to hear someone extend him grace on this.

Tessa was suddenly struck by the most extraordinary detail. "You have her eyes," she said with a gentle wonder in her voice.

"That can't be good."

"No, really, it is. I would never have seen it before, but you do. Hers are mostly squinting and glaring, but the shape and the color are the same. I like your eyes." That felt weirdly intimate to admit. "I guess that means Norma had lovely eyes as a young woman." Tessa set her elbows on the table. "Wow, that is crazy to imagine. Norma Binton in a torrid romance. It boggles the mind."

"Now you see why I can't exactly saunter up to her at the drugstore and reveal myself as the walking embodiment of her darkest secret." The profound disappointment of it all pulled the light from his eyes and slumped his shoulders.

"I'm sorry, really." Tessa could only imagine what it would be like to anticipate meeting your birth mother and then finding out she was a woman most people disliked. What had it been like to stand at the dessert table at the barbecue and talk about something as mundane as pie? No wonder he'd looked shell-shocked most of the evening. "Do you think you will ever? Tell her?" Tessa had to admit, there wasn't a lot of reason to think it would go well. Maybe there really were some secrets best left alone.

"I don't know." Neal sank back in his chair. "It feels weird to have someone else know. That's the first time I've ever said it out loud."

"You can trust me," she felt compelled to reassure him. "I won't tell a soul until you're ready. If you're ever ready. Please don't regret telling me. I understand everything so much better now that I know." A sense of honor welled up in her, to hold this secret for him. It seemed another reason why Tessa was coming to feel that it had been no accident he'd rented the house next door, no coincidence that he was there now. *What are You up to, Lord?*

she prayed as she set the coffees down in front of them. *What am I doing in the middle of this? Help me do the right thing here.*

"Could you really leave without telling her?" she asked gently. "Wouldn't it just always be hanging out there if you don't? I know it might be awful, but at least then you'd know. You'd both know."

"Maybe." He stared into his coffee as if it were a deep abyss. "Part of me feels that way. Some wounds will always fester if you don't open them up and clean them."

If a human being could be a festering wound, they probably would look and act like Norma Binton. That brought up a surprising possibility. "What if you were just that? What if meeting you is the thing that heals Norma?"

Neal almost rolled his eyes. "That's being rather optimistic, don't you think?"

"I admit, it's a stretch. A big one. But Pastor Newton always says God is in the surprise business. I can't think of a bigger surprise than what you've got to say to Norma." When Neal looked skeptical, she added, "Why would God let you come this far only to go back to Minneapolis with the same hurt? If she's terrible, you're still in the same spot. If she's open, if she's even the tiniest bit better by knowing, isn't that worth a shot? For both of you?"

"You really can be pushy, you know that?" He was only half teasing.

"I know I have no right to tell you what to do here. But I've never felt it was dumb luck that you rented Valerie's house just as the kittens arrived." Tessa risked putting her hand over his. "I'm glad you're here. I'm glad I know. And I will help in any way I can, even if it's just to talk it out. Whatever you decide to do, you don't have to do it alone."

He gave her a warm, sad smile that made Tessa regret the end of his month was fifteen days away. Neal was an astounding man. She cared about him, cared *for* him. But for all her optimism, he was right about one thing; this story wasn't likely to have a happy ending.

Only a God-sized dose of grace and mercy would keep Neal from going home to Minnesota rejected by Norma and out of her life forever.

Neal tamped down his nerves as he sat across the lunch table from Pastor Newton. They were sitting in the dining room of the cleverly named Wander Inn after the pastor had called to invite him to lunch.

"Did Tessa put you up to this?" While Neal's gut told him he could trust Tessa, he still felt wildly exposed that she knew his secret. Still, it was comforting on some level to see her shock and dismay at the prospect of Norma being his birth mother. The bitter old woman seemed such an unlikely—and disheartening—candidate. Honestly, some part of him hoped it might not be true. That he'd somehow identified the wrong woman.

The pastor laughed. "I'll admit, that

does sound like something Tessa would do. But no, this was all my idea."

"Why?" Neal had gone to the same big church in Minneapolis for almost three years and no pastor had ever asked him to lunch there.

The reverend scanned the menu as he spoke. "We're not exactly a tourist town. Oh, we get a few folks in from the golf resort, but that's mostly lunch and shopping, or the carousel. Someone staying for a month is unusual. Someone coming to church their first weekend in town is unusual, too. Plus—" he looked up and leaned in "—I'm thinking about one of those kittens. And if I even breathe a word of that to Tessa, we both know what will happen. I figured I was safer inquiring with you."

Neal wasn't quite sure what to make of that answer. "The kittens seem to be in good shape, mostly. Then there's that little one. I think he'll make it. Tessa's sure going to do everything she can to ensure that he does." His memory brought up the image of Tessa feeding the tiny thing, saying soft, encouraging words, pouring so much love into little Charlie.

"Tessa has one of the biggest hearts in Wander Canyon," Newton said after they'd ordered with the server. "She's been a good friend to lots of people. Did you have fun at the barbecue?"

Now, that was a complicated question. He'd enjoyed the food, the atmosphere, and when he was honest with himself, he enjoyed Tessa's company a great deal. But *fun* wasn't quite the word. Neal settled for saying, "You all sure know how to eat."

"My family's secret rib recipe does tend to bring folks out. But I think we'd have the same kind of event eating peanut butter and jelly sandwiches. This town likes to gather and celebrate—even if they're celebrating nothing in particular."

They made more small talk as a pair of hefty sandwiches and homemade coleslaw came to the table. The grace the pastor said over their meal was simple and heart-felt. A few bites into the meal, however, Pastor Newton gave Neal a direct look and said, "I can't help thinking you're in town for more than just rest and relaxation."

Neal felt his breath hitch. "Why's that?" He'd tried to be so careful and casual in his interactions with everyone.

Newton shook his head. "Pastoral radar, I suppose. You strike me as a man with a lot to work out. Needing a lot of space to work it out in."

Neal thought about dismissing the comment, but opted for cautious honesty. "I'm working through some things."

"Good spot to do it in. A glorious hunk of creation like these mountains does lend a certain perspective. And a good chunk of time is always wise. I'm a fan of long walks and good views when I need to solve a problem."

"I mostly run," Neal said. "Clears my head." Only he wasn't any clearer right now on what to do about Norma Binton than when he'd first arrived. If anything, he was less certain of his next steps.

"Well, if there's any way I can help, I hope you'll..."

"Dr. Rodgers!" The little boy Neal recognized as Cole from his earlier trip to The Depot burst through the door with his father, Jake, close behind. "One of the eggs hatched! We got our first baby turtle!"

"Sorry to interrupt," Jake said. "Cole saw you through the window and he was dying to tell you."

"It's amazing," Cole said with wide eyes. "And there are two more that'll come soon."

Neal liked the feel of the easy smile that came to his face. "Sounds like you took excellent care of your pets."

"Dad and Emmom say I can keep them. I can adopt the baby turtles like they adopted me. Isn't that cool? Five whole turtles." Cole's chest swelled with pride.

"Jake adopted his nephew when his

sister and her husband passed away. 'Emmom' is Jake's wife, Emma," Pastor Newton said by way of explanation. The reverend beamed up at Jake. "Your family is one of my favorite Wander Canyon happy endings."

"I was adopted, too," Neal surprised himself by saying. "Those little turtles are going to have a great home with you."

"You were?" Cole asked. "So you had a Gotcha Day, too?"

Neal laughed. "I don't think we called it that, but we should have. Do you celebrate it?"

"Every year," Jake said. "Cake and everything. Why have one day with cake and candles when you can have two?"

"Like I said," Pastor Newton agreed, "one of my favorite happy endings. Now with more turtles, too."

"We have another big announcement," Cole said, his young voice trying to sound important. He tugged on his father's arm and grinned.

"I've decided to run for mayor of Wander Canyon," Jake announced, catching the ear of several people at nearby tables.

"*Mayor* Dad," Cole pronounced, as if the election were already decided. He looked at Neal. "You can't vote, though. Only people who live here can."

"That's too bad," Neal teased, slightly amazed at the lightness he felt around these people. "I think those five turtles are a pretty solid endorsement."

Jake laughed. "Maybe I should work that into a campaign speech. 'Five out of five turtles recommend Jake Sanders for mayor.'"

The reverend shook Jake's hand. "That's wonderful. I'm glad to see you taking on a new challenge like that. So many people your age don't think about how they can give back to the town."

"Wander's given a lot to me," Jake replied. "Enjoy your lunch. Sorry again to interrupt."

"Happy news like that is no interruption

at all," Pastor Newton replied. He smiled and shook his head as Jake and Cole left and he returned to his meal. "Five turtles. Maybe I should look into one of them instead of a kitten."

"Kittens are better company. But don't tell Cole I said that." Neal's eyes were drawn out the restaurant window to watch the duo now walking hand in hand down the street. Cole chattered happily while Jake nodded with love and attention.

He had lots of similar memories with his father, who had adopted him with as much love as Jake clearly had for his nephew. *I ought to remember that more. Life gave me way more love than loss. I was never alone.*

The image of Norma sitting solitary and rigid in the front pew poked its way into his mind. Norma Binton looked very alone. He waited for a glimpse of pity, a sense of compassion, to come from the lonely image, but felt mostly numb. There was more resentment festering under the surface than he'd realized. Yeah, he was working through some things. Big things.

"You were adopted?" The pastor's question pulled Neal back to the present.

"As a baby. My adoptive parents gave me a wonderful life." It bothered Neal how he seemed to need to emphasize that lately.

"It's a true blessing when that happens. Jake and Emma have been so careful to keep the memory of Cole's parents alive for him." He sighed. "We all miss Natalie and Kurt very much. The accident that killed them was a huge tragedy for our town." Returning to his sandwich, he asked, "Have you ever met your birth parents? Know anything about them? That seems to happen so much more these days."

Shouldn't someone like a pastor have a better sense of what a huge question that was? He asked so casually, not at all like he was ripping open a massive wound. Then again, how could he know?

"No," Neal said, trying to match the pastor's casual tone. Something in Pastor Newton's eyes told him he'd failed.

"Not everyone feels the need. Or even has access to the information. I'm glad to hear you had such a wonderful childhood." He pointed at Neal with a potato chip. "It shows in how you care for people, by the way. Just now with Cole. And Molly Bradshaw went on and on to me the other day about how great you were with Zack at the barbecue. I expect whoever it was that gave you birth would be proud to see the good man you are today."

Neal had to swallow hard to fight the surge of emotion welling up at such a compliment. *If you only knew,* he thought. He'd have to tell Tessa about this conversation when he got back to the house. It *was* a good thing Tessa knew. It felt less daunting to know he didn't have to work things out all by himself.

Chapter Twelve

Tessa, Zack and Molly sat on a blanket inside a large octagonal pen where the kittens played. The Monday afternoon sunshine and warm weather made it a pleasant task to sit with Zack as he considered each of the unclaimed kittens. And Molly was a good friend, so it was a chance to catch up on everything that had happened since the barbecue.

"Little Charlie's doing better?" Molly asked.

"Gaining weight a little bit every day. I have to supplement the weak nursing he's doing with bottle feeding, which is a bit of a challenge." Tessa leaned in toward her friend. "But then again, when aren't boys a challenge?"

Molly raised an eyebrow. "Are we still talking about kittens?"

Tessa sat back on her elbows as Patsy decided to play tug-of-war with the leg of her jeans. "I'm not sure," she laughed to her friend. The kitten tumbled over herself comically as she swatted at the fraying hem. Tessa jiggled her leg just a bit, and Patsy pounced.

The sight made Molly laugh as well. "Everything okay with Greg? He still having loads of fun out in Utah?"

Tessa sent up another small prayer of thanks that these kittens had come into her life. They were such a welcome distraction. "I may or may not have sulked that someone missed his weekly phone call again Saturday night." She sighed. "I don't know whether to call Nick on it or just be happy Greg is having too much fun to remember to call home."

Zack giggled from the other side of the pen as he lay on his back and three of the kittens began climbing all over his stomach. Zack had his challenges, but he was such a sweet boy. Greg had been a sweet boy at that age, too. That boy was still in there, right? Hiding under the grumpy teenager who usually answered any questions in single words like *fine*, *good*, *nothing* and *okay*.

"Maybe you can just be grateful that Nick is still at least willing to have some kind of father-son relationship with Greg." Molly's voice held a touch of regret. Her split from Zack's father had been as heartbreaking as Tessa's own divorce. Both women had fought to save their marriage with a man who simply was no longer interested in fighting to fix it.

"I know I should be glad," Tessa admitted. "I'm just worried that it's looking far more like fun buddy than responsible parent." She sat back up. "Greg texted me a photo of himself on an ATV, looking thrilled, and do you know I couldn't stop myself from texting back 'Are you wearing a helmet?'"

Molly offered a smirk of sympathy. "Was he?"

"Yes, but now I look like a total nag instead of someone glad he's having fun."

Molly picked up Patsy from her ongoing attack of Tessa's pant leg. "The problem is you've just had too much wonderful parenting. Your mom and dad are some of the best parents I know. That sets a high bar."

Tessa's thoughts cast back to the mystery of the baptismal entry. She did have wonderful parents. Why was she letting some innocent detail fester in her mind like this? She felt a faint echo of the weight Neal carried, knowing a secret but not yet ready to share it with anyone. Only, he had shared his with her, and it bound them together in ways that made Tessa think that maybe she could share her questions with Neal. He would understand, and the fact that he was outside the Wander community would mean no harm would be done if there was nothing at all to her curiosity. Because it was nothing, right? She was avoiding talking to her parents about it for no good reason. Reading way too much into a simple change of ink and a set of dates.

"Test-driving a few of the kittens?" Neal's voice from behind them drew Tessa from her thoughts.

"He's asleep on me," Zack said in a loud whisper as he pointed to Blake now happily napping on his chest. "I think he likes me."

"Looks that way to me." Neal squatted just outside the pen. "Sometimes you choose the pet, and sometimes the pet chooses you."

Zack turned toward his mom with an adorable hope in his eyes. "Do you think he chose me, Mom?"

Tessa grinned as she watched Molly nod to Zack. Making decisions was hard for a boy with Zack's anxieties. Why wouldn't

God work it out so little Blake made the decision easy by choosing for him? The little gray kitten looked totally at home on Zack's chest, purring as Zack gently rubbed his back. "What do you think you'll name him, Zack?" The idea that another of the kittens had found a wonderful home made her heart glow.

As expected, Zack had given this a lot of thought. "It can't be a big change 'cause he's used to Blake. Since he's gray, I thought I could call him Smoke. What do you think, Dr. Rodgers?"

"It's a fine and thoughtful name."

"But he can't leave his mama just yet," Molly reminded Zack. "He's not old enough."

"I know." Zack nearly pouted. "Can I come back and see him again, Miss Tessa?"

He looked so happy to know the kitten would be his. "Anytime you like, Zack. Consider Blake—or Smoke—yours until he can go home with you for good."

"Hooray!" the little boy cheered as he

gently placed the sleeping kitten back among his brothers and sisters on the blanket.

Tessa hoped Neal didn't catch the wink Molly sent her way as she gathered up Zack. "Let's get going. I promise we'll come back soon."

"That's four down, three to go, right?" Neal said as Molly and Zack headed back to their car.

Tessa was impressed he'd been keeping track. "It is."

Neal stepped over the pen to squat inside, smiling as two of the kittens came right up to say hello. "You might have another one gone soon."

"Are you thinking of taking one?" She hadn't expected that.

He shook his head. "Oh, no. But Pastor Newton is thinking about it. He told me so at lunch."

"You had lunch with Pastor Newton?" She'd been wondering where he'd been heading off to when he walked down the street two hours ago. Not that she would ever admit to watching his comings and goings. The man was entitled to his privacy, after all—even from snooping neighbors who were struggling with finding him increasingly attractive.

"He invited me when I was in The Depot after a run yesterday. I thought it'd be rude to say no."

"That's nice of him." It *was* kind of Pastor Newton to reach out to Neal, him being a visitor and all. And certainly like the pastor to do something like that. Tessa found herself just a tiny bit disappointed Neal hadn't told her about the invitation—which was silly. If her goal was to introduce him to lots of Wander Canyon residents, why was she miffed that he was meeting them on his own? It wasn't very attractive, or charitable, she chided herself. "He can absolutely have one of the kittens."

When she realized Neal had settled himself on the grass beside the pen, Tessa drove the conversation a bit further. "What did you talk about?"

"My adoption."

That stunned her. Pastor Newton had a way of getting people to open up, but getting Neal to talk about his adoption was a feat even for the likes of the reverend's pastoral skills. "Really? You told him about...her?" Even though they were alone in the yard, she didn't feel she had the right to use Norma's name. The secret still felt enormous and binding between them.

"No. I'm not ready for anyone to know that. Anyone but you, I mean."

The way he said that sneaked its way inside Tessa. She watched him as he told her about seeing Cole and Jake, and talking about his own parents. His words softened as he spoke, as if seeing a happy family like Cole, Jake and Emma could help to heal the wounds he was discovering Norma had left. Parenting could be both a blessing and a struggle. No one could love you like your parents—but no one could wound you like them as well.

He grew silent for a moment, laughing quietly at how Patsy swatted at a blade of grass he dangled above her head. Tessa had never met a man who could be so dark and yet so tender at the same time. Did secrets make you that way? Despite digging into facts and deceptions professionally, she'd never felt the shadow of any secrets cross her life.

Until now. Now the intriguing detail of her baptismal entry in the church ledger poked at her like an insistent toddler.

"Tessa?" His voice called her back from her thoughts. "Where'd you go just now?"

Something had changed in her. One of the things that had drawn him most to her was how present she was. How "in the moment" she could be. Neal hadn't felt as if he were grounded anywhere lately, and Tessa seemed effortlessly grounded to this place and these people...until now.

Maybe she was just frustrated with her writing project. "How's the history research coming?" He wanted to see the sparkle return to her eyes. He was becoming rather fond of that sparkle, unwise as it was for a man whose vacation was halfway finished.

"Okay," she said. He could tell instantly that it wasn't true. She chewed on her lower lip, deciding whether to tell him something. Neal wasn't sure what to do with how easily he seemed to be able to read her feelings. He held her gaze for longer than he should, hoping it invited her to share more.

Tessa sat up and hugged her knees. Neal didn't like the side of the pen between them—he longed to climb in there with her and the kittens, but it seemed such an absurd thing to do. So, he simply placed one hand on the top of the pen, leaning over on the excuse of playing with Patsy when really he just wanted to be closer to Tessa and the worry in her eyes.

"It's silly," she said, waving one hand as if she could bat whatever thought troubled her away the way Patsy batted at the grass blade.

"Doesn't look like it is to me," he said. "Tell me." When that felt entirely too close, he rushed to add, "You already know my darkest secret. It's okay if I know one of yours." He tried to make it sound like a joke, but it didn't quite come out that way. After all, he didn't know if it was a secret that was bothering her, except that the tension he sensed from her felt so familiar.

"I'm sure I'm just imagining things," she persisted, and he knew then that whatever was hounding her wasn't small at all. After all, he knew too well what it sounded like when you were trying to talk yourself into ignoring something.

"Tell me," he repeated. He reached out and touched her shoulder. What he really wanted to do was take her hand.

"Pastor Newton gave me a bunch of

baptismal ledgers to go through for my research. They're all these wonderful old handwritten records of when babies were born and baptized into the church. Tons of details and names and dates. I found my great-grandfather and my grandfather and even my mom and dad. We go back a bunch of generations in these parts."

She was trying to tell him everything but the thing that was bothering her. Years of listening to people talk about their pets had given him a strong sense of what people *weren't* saying. He kept silent, letting her work up to it, whatever it was.

"I followed the trail all the way up to my own baptism. Back in the eighties, before Pastor Newton was at the church. There's a photo of it on my parents' mantel." She straightened, chin up. "I was an adorable baby, you know."

She was dodging again, but he found himself smiling. "I don't doubt it for a minute." He found her adorable now, although the word didn't do a woman of her vibrancy justice. Kittens were adorable. Tessa was…captivating.

"There was just something weird about the entry." Her hands returned to hugging her knees—tighter this time. "I'm sure I'm seeing things that aren't there. Occupational hazard for journalists."

"What'd you see?"

"My dad's name. It was…different. A different ink color, like it hadn't been filled in with the other stuff." She paused, hung up on the detail. He knew that feeling, as if something had you by the leg and wouldn't let you walk farther on. "It's stupid, like I said. There could be a million reasons why it's that way. I'm… It's… a dumb detail."

She blinked and swallowed hard. It wasn't just a dumb detail. It was eating away at her, imagined or not.

"You know," he said as gently as he could, "you can do the one thing I can't. You can ask."

"No, I can't," she shot back quickly.

"How could I ask about something like that? What am I supposed to ask?"

It really was taking an effort not to climb in there beside her. "You don't have to imply anything. Couldn't you show them the entry and ask why it looks the way it does?" He shrugged. "Maybe they have a funny story about how the pastor misspelled your dad's name or the ink ran out."

"Misspelled *Benjamin*?" He imagined the incredulous look she gave him had put Greg in his place more than once.

"Okay, maybe not that. But you said so yourself—there's probably an innocent explanation. Just ask them."

"They'll think I'm questioning things. Questioning Dad. I can't do that. I'd rather not know than ask them that."

Neal fixed her with the strongest gaze he dared. "'I'd rather not know' is a lie. I, of all people, know that. It'll eat at you."

"It's nothing," she insisted.

"No, it's not." It was the furthest thing

from nothing, no matter what you told yourself. These past few days had shown him that in ways he couldn't have imagined.

She looked at him, and he could see the uprooted feeling that had been his constant companion this past year reflected in her eyes. "You're pushy, you know that?"

He liked that she used his own words. "I've had a very good role model recently."

"This does not get to turn into 'if I ask her, you have to ask him.' That's not how this goes."

He hadn't realized until just this moment how much he wanted to be there for her. In this, with Charlie, even with Greg. He hated the idea of life squashing that great big heart of hers. It mattered to him—way more than it should—that she should be happy. He wanted to live in a world where Tessa Kennedy was cared for in return just as fiercely as she cared.

But he was leaving. Despite any hopes he'd foolishly mustered up, he knew there was no reconciliation coming from Norma. Oh, he'd say his piece with the woman for the consolation of knowing he'd tried, for the satisfaction of bringing the truth to light. But nothing would come of it. She'd be hurt, and offended, and bitter, leaving him with no real reason to return and a hundred reasons to stay away.

As much as being there for Tessa pulled at him, all he had to offer her was the next two weeks. That meant he had nothing to offer her.

But that did little to stop him from wanting to. He held Tessa's eyes for a long moment, searching for some way to say everything that shouldn't be said. There was a flicker of a moment where a reckless urge to hold her in his arms took hold, where her eyes almost convinced him to make assurances he couldn't possibly keep. Instead, he gripped the side of the pen and stared at the ground, a coward pretending to play with kittens.

Send her someone she can truly lean

on. It was a moment or two before he realized the thought was actually a prayer.
Send her someone, because it can't be me.

Chapter Thirteen

Some people worked out their problems behind a fishing pole, some on a golf course or in their yard. Neal worked out his problems under the hood of his car. So while there was nothing especially in need of repair at the moment, Neal found himself wandering the automotive aisle of the local hardware store, hoping inspiration would hit him.

"Car guy, huh?" said a voice to his left just beyond the detail brushes and waxes. Neal turned to find Dr. Davidson, the local veterinarian.

"Since I was old enough to drive. Before that, even."

Dr. Davidson offered a knowing smirk. "I had a poster of a Camaro up on my wall before I could see over the steering wheel. And about a thousand Matchbox cars. I keep half of 'em, hoping my grandsons will catch the bug, but they seem more interested in buttons and joysticks than gearshifts and spark plugs."

Neal's memory brought up the image of his father pushing a step stool up to the hood of the family car, patiently explaining the parts and how they worked as Neal leaned over to soak it all in. "My dad says I was born with grease under my fingernails." He didn't like the way saying "my dad" suddenly snagged in his chest lately. Luke Rodgers *was* his dad. It wasn't fair to let biology dampen the wonderful relationship he had with the man who was the only father he'd ever known. "I'm a vet and a car guy because of him."

"That pretty blue number in the parking lot belong to you?" Davidson looked impressed.

"It does." Lots of people thought Neal's Chrysler was snazzy, but the admiration of another car enthusiast was always welcome praise. "What do you drive?"

Davidson sighed. "Nothing fancy anymore. I'm gearing up to retire down to the coast. Gonna learn to be a boat guy."

Tessa had said he was retiring. Or that he seemed to be ready to. The man did have a weary look to him. Neal nodded, not really knowing how to respond.

"Little Charlie hanging in there? Gaining?"

Neal shrugged. "Seems to be. I think the little fellow knows better than to disappoint the likes of Tessa."

Davidson chuckled. "All those kittens. I told her they wouldn't all likely make it, but she just seemed to take that as a dare. I hope she's right."

"She's up to the challenge, I think."

Davidson inspected a can of tire cleaner. "I've been meaning to ask you. How'd you swing a whole month away from your practice? Got a partner?"

Desperation, Neal thought to himself. *Exhaustion.* "I called in a few favors and took on an associate for what I couldn't cover elsewhere." He heard the echo of his tech's worried voice as she'd chided him one night, saying, "Go fix what's wrong with you." What would happen to him if he came back from this trip no better than when he'd left? Could he keep going? Would it be worse? This wasn't like a car, where if you just kept tinkering and adjusting, you could eventually get it to run.

"Can I buy you lunch and you can tell me how you set it up?" the older man asked. "I'm worried about what will happen here when I pull up stakes." Neal looked at the man's weary expression and wondered if he was looking at his future. He couldn't imagine a time where he'd be too tired to care, and at the same time he felt the resignation creeping up on him.

"It's different in a city like Minneapolis. People have other places they can go."

"That's just it," Davidson said, pressing his lips together as he returned the can to the shelf. "Around here, I'm it. Well, for everything other than livestock, at least." He hesitated, tucking his hands in his pockets and rocking back on his heels. Neal braced himself for what he knew was coming. "Don't suppose you'd like the canyon well enough to consider staying?"

"Not possible," Neal replied, despite the surprising lure of the idea. He wouldn't leave without revealing himself to Norma, and he couldn't stay once she rejected him. That left no options where Davidson's offer made any kind of sense. "I'm sure you can find someone. This is such a nice little town."

Davidson shook his head. "No one your age is looking for nice little towns these days. My best hope is to get someone a bit younger than me and hope Wander keeps 'em for five or six years at most." He raised an eyebrow. "You know anyone?"

"I'll think about it," Neal said, just because he knew Davidson was right. It would be hard to get someone young in to a small practice like that. A vet would have to have other reasons to say yes to Wander Canyon.

And Neal was pretty sure he was not going to have any of those.

Tessa took a big swig of iced tea and typed "Dawson Porterfield" into the denominational website. It felt like cheating. Tessa didn't even know if the pastor who'd signed her baptismal record was even alive, much less where he lived. He certainly had to be retired. This was a wild-goose chase, to be sure.

Still, chasing Pastor Porterfield down felt like less of a hurdle than asking her parents about it. Or even Pastor Newton. It would look so foolish if it was nothing. She'd hurt them just by asking, just by what asking them would imply. *Oh, by the way, Mom and Dad, anything you want to tell me about my birth and baptism? Any tiny details you might have left out?*

She was ashamed how a shift in ink color and an unusual delay in dates could uproot her sense of stability like this. Neal's history had her spooked, that was all. "This is the best option," she assured Charlie, currently curled in her lap as if he'd always belonged there. The healthy curve of the kitten's belly was her favorite victory of late. Charlie was going to make it. She wouldn't accept any other outcome.

She clicked the button to begin a search, relieved when it brought up the classification of retired rather than deceased or unknown. It listed his last-known position in a church an hour north of here. "That's doable," she proclaimed to Charlie's yellow eyes. "I mean, this isn't the kind of thing you can do by email, right?"

Reporters were skilled at tracking down people, so it wasn't long before Tessa had an address and a phone number.

"Hello?" came an older female voice on the phone.

"I'm a volunteer from Wander Canyon Community Church. I'm looking for Reverend Porterfield."

"Oh, we haven't been back to Wander in years. He's out in the garden. Let me go get him."

"I'm doing some historical research," she said when the reverend came on the phone. "I've got a bunch of records from when you were pastor here. Do you think I could come up your way tomorrow and ask a few questions?" One giant question, actually. But there were also plenty of historical details she wanted to explore if that one giant question turned out to be a dud, so her inquiry wasn't untrue. It was just a bit...incomplete.

Tessa was grateful he agreed easily. "I think I can manage that. My memory isn't as sharp as it used to be, but I'll do my best to help."

"Much appreciated," Tessa said. Relief and anxiety clashed in the pit of her stomach at the prospect of getting to an answer so quickly.

"What did you say your name was, dear?" He sounded so kind. Like everybody's favorite grandfather.

"Tessa," she said, momentarily grateful she'd gone by Theresa when she was younger, shortening it to Tessa after she'd married Nick. She was even more grateful when Porterfield didn't ask her last name.

"Well, Tessa, we'll see you tomorrow."

Dawson Porterfield had been very well-liked. She'd heard that from more than one longtime WCCC member old enough to remember the years before Pastor Newton. A painting of Porterfield even hung in the preschool library. He'd left when she was still young—Tessa had no real memory of him. It would be an honor to meet him, to hear his stories, she told herself. She didn't have to make this all about one tiny detail that might prove to be irrelevant.

She knew one thing instantly: she didn't want to do this alone. She didn't want to mull it over the whole drive up so that she was in a state by the time she met Reverend Porterfield. And she wanted someone to talk over what she found if it was huge. Because it might very well be huge.

That meant, unless she was willing to reveal this to someone else, there was only one person she could ask. So when his car pulled into the driveway, that was exactly what she did.

"That's such a gorgeous car," she said, starting off with a compliment. "Is it as much fun to drive as it looks?"

He grinned. "Most days." He raised an eyebrow. "Do you want to take it for a spin?"

Tessa hadn't expected that offer. Neal

clearly loved that car. "You don't really let other people drive it, do you?"

He leaned back against the side of the car, looking every bit like a magazine ad. "Well, no, but maybe I should."

She laughed. "Well, I don't think you should start with me. Besides, I can't drive stick, and I'm pretty sure that's not the car I should learn on."

"Probably not."

Tessa suddenly felt sheepish. It was just a drive—and probably a scenic one at that. "But… I was wondering if you'd like to drive me somewhere. You know, a bit of a road trip."

He had every reason to look confused. After all, she was a grown woman perfectly capable of driving herself anywhere she chose.

"I found the pastor who signed my baptismal record. I want to go ask him about it, and he lives about an hour from here."

She should have expected the dubious look he gave her. "Your parents are ten minutes down the road." She regretted telling him that, but in Wander Canyon, wasn't everybody ten minutes down the road?

"I know that," she replied. "I'm just not ready to ask them about it. Especially if it's nothing—which I'm sure it is. It's easier this way."

"I'm not so sure I agree." But, after a moment's hesitation, he said, "Sure, I'll drive you. When?"

"Tomorrow. You're free? I mean...you're on vacation, so you're free, right?"

"Even if I weren't, I'd make time."

Neal luxuriated in the way the car hugged the steep mountain curve. This part of the country was filled with breathtaking drives—why hadn't he done this earlier?

He stole a glimpse over at Tessa, lost in thought as the wind from the open window tossed her hair. She'd chattered nervously the whole first part of the drive, but now she'd fallen into a thoughtful silence.

He knew that feeling—sorting through everything you thought you knew, wondering how much of it would stand past the conversation you were about to have. He'd been in that continual state of what-if since his arrival in Wander Canyon. Still was. And he would be until he took the huge risk of telling Norma Binton he was her son. He was just so sure it would hurt—badly—that he couldn't bring himself to do it yet.

"What will you do if he tells you something?" he dared to ask, hoping to bring her back to the present. She was sitting right next to him in the car and yet he missed her on account of how distant she was.

She turned to him, biting her thumbnail. The gesture made her look so young. Vulnerable, looking for assurance. It called to his protective nature the way she had that first morning when she'd banged in kitten-panic on his door. "I'm not sure," she said. "It doesn't change anything, and yet it could change everything."

He worked up the nerve to ask the question that had been on his mind for the last dozen miles. "What do you think it means? The ink change, the length between the dates. I mean, if you were a reporter looking into this, and it wasn't your entry, what would you think it meant?" He had an idea where her mind was heading, but it could be his own sharp bias talking.

Tessa took in a deep breath. "I'd think it meant there was some reason why they left it blank at first. Some reason why they waited between the birth and the baptism."

"Like..."

"It could be any number of things. Grandma or Grandpa was sick. A burst pipe at the church. I was sick. Or Mom. Or Dad." She paused, and he knew she was deciding whether or not to say it. If he'd considered it a possibility, he knew she must have. "Or..."

Neal remained silent, letting her work

her way into the thought. She was thinking it so loud—if that was a thing—it was practically louder than the hum of the car engine. It might help her to say it. Maybe she'd hear the absurdity of it, how unlikely it was, if she said it out loud.

"Or there was some reason they didn't want to write my dad's name in on that blank. At first or…at all."

"Do you think that's really possible?" The loving way Tessa described her parents, Neal didn't think so. Even his own parents had told him the truth of his adoption as early as he could understand it, how God sent him to his mother and father, how he was the answer to so, so many prayers. He didn't see how people who loved Tessa that much would keep such a thing from her. That was something people did back in the fifties, back when no one was willing to admit children came into the world in less-than-ideal ways.

Then again, it was what Norma had done, wasn't it?

"I mean, I know I'm my mom's child. Come on—look at this hair." The wild waves of her hair did make her adorable. And those dimples when she smiled. "But what if my dad...isn't my dad?"

"You're drawing a lot of conclusions from a few minor details, don't you think? Maybe the pen ran out."

She narrowed her eyes at him. "The blank for father's name comes before the blank for mother's name. Nice try."

He pointed to the sign that said they were entering the town. "We're almost here. You know, he may not remember," Neal offered. "He must have baptized hundreds of babies."

He shouldn't have been surprised that she'd thought of that. "That'll tell me there isn't anything remarkable. I don't think pastors forget stuff like this, even after a long time. If there was drama involved in my baptism, he'll remember."

"But he may not tell you. He may think that this is something you should hear from your own parents."

She sulked a bit at that, then asked, "Did you hear it from yours?"

"It's not quite the same thing, but yes. They told me as early as they could, with a lot of honesty and love."

"Were you shocked?"

It was odd that he'd never stopped to think about it. "I suppose I was. I mostly remember looking in the mirror and thinking 'Well, that explains the hair.'"

Neal was glad to hear her laugh at that. "Huh?"

"Mom has red hair and Dad is a blond. Although, Mom told me stories of people coming up to her and saying, 'Oh, he looks so much like you.' She'd always laugh and say, 'Really?' She used to joke that if people could end up looking like their pets, couldn't children grow into looking like their parents? To this day she insists I learned my scowl from my dad."

"He must have had quite a scowl."

He'd managed to pull her from her fearful thoughts, which was good, because he turned down the street and into the driveway of the quaint little house three doors down. "We're here."

"We're here," she said, sounding scared.

"It's better to know," he reassured her, even though he wasn't sure she was going to come away from today knowing anything. Except maybe that there was nothing to know. Just an ink color and a date, nothing more.

She grabbed the tote bag of old ledgers from the floor by her feet. "You're going to come in with me, aren't you?"

He'd hoped to, but didn't want to intrude. He was happy enough just to be the ride there and back, but willing to do more. "If that's what you want."

"That's absolutely what I want. So you're a church volunteer, just like me, got it?"

He applied his father's famous scowl. "You're going to lie to a man of God?"

"Only at first. I didn't think he'd let me come if he knew the real question I was asking." She opened the car door and got out.

"You're making way more of this than you need to," he said as he got out from behind the wheel.

She looked at him from over the hood. "Let's hope that's true."

Chapter Fourteen

$\sim$

Tessa had a whole list of questions in her notebook, but they all tangled up in her head as she settled on the couch opposite Dawson Porterfield and his very friendly wife, Ginny. The couple had to be in their late eighties, old and creaky, but with lively eyes. When she saw the pastor, it lit a vague memory of him as a younger man making visits to the preschool she'd attended as a child.

Did the sight of her face pull up a memory? Tessa held on tightly to the stack of ledgers in her lap in an effort to stop her hands from fidgeting.

He folded his hands in his lap. "So, young lady, what is it you want to know?"

She couldn't just start with what she really wanted to know. "I'm working on a project. A history of Wander Canyon and the families who settled the town. It might be a book. Someday, maybe. Right now, I'm just trying to make sense of a bunch of research. Starting with wedding and baptismal records."

The pastor smiled. "Happy events. They were always my favorite."

"Except for the barbecue," Ginny said, laying a hand on his elbow in the way long-married couples did—the way Mom did so often to Dad. "Do they still do the summer barbecue?"

"Just last week," Tessa replied. "And I imagine it's still as good as you remember it."

"And services on the lawn some Sundays," Ginny went on. "With lemonade. Do they still do that?"

"Once a month, as soon as it turns warm

enough." It felt good to give the Porter-fields some happy reassurances that his beloved congregation was still alive and healthy. The trip didn't feel so much as if it was all about getting something from him this way.

"Who's your young man here?" Ginny said with the hint of a wink in her eye.

"This is Neal. He's a..." She suddenly couldn't come up with the right word for what Neal was. She settled on saying, "Friend. He drove me up here today."

Porterfield peered through the window behind where they sat on the couch. "That's a beauty of a car you've got there, son."

"Thanks."

"So," Tessa said, trying not to take a deep breath or show any of the nerves clanging up and down her spine. She flipped open the first two ledgers and laid them open on the coffee table, picking up a notebook where she'd written down some innocuous facts. "You were pastor from '78 to '86, so the weddings in here are from before you." She pointed to the first ledger. "As well as the baptisms in here," she added, pointing to the second ledger.

"I was Wander Canyon Community Church's third pastor. And the first one to hire a secretary."

"There was a time when the pastor's wife was expected to do that sort of thing, but I was already a teacher and we had two children in school," Ginny added.

"But you started the preschool, didn't you?"

"I hired Norma Binton as our first teacher, yes."

Tessa felt Neal react beside her. Just a slight tensing of his shoulders, nothing Reverend Porterfield would notice, surely. Tessa tried to picture Norma cheerfully tending to little preschoolers, and couldn't quite do it. "She's still on the board of the school, actually."

"Is she? She was always so serious about

her job. Serious about everything, now that I think about it." There seemed to be a story there, and Tessa paused, giving Neal a chance to ask a question if he wanted to. He remained silent, but she noticed his hand tightened against his knee.

"Did you have a favorite wedding? One that would make a good story?" She'd written that question down so that the conversation wouldn't sound like the fact hunt it really was.

"Oh, Don and Irene Redding's. That's one for a history book." Porterfield chuckled to himself.

"Toni's mom and dad?" Tessa asked. It made for the perfect excuse to open the other set of ledgers of weddings and baptisms—the ones from Porterfield's years as pastor. The ones with her in them.

Ginny laughed. "Oh, the rain. The church basement flooded and two of the sanctuary windows broke. We ended up having to move the whole thing to Carlson's barn. Irene was in such a state, but Don thought it was nothing at all."

"Until one of the cattle walked in toward the end of the ceremony." Reverend Porterfield laughed so hard, he had to wipe his eyes. "I thought the mother of the bride was going to faint." He tucked his handkerchief back in his pocket. "I hear Hank Walker married again, too. That's nice to hear. News doesn't always make it up to us, you know. I'll have to read your book when you write it."

The reverend looked at her for a moment, and Tessa felt her stomach drop. "Did I baptize you? You look about the right age, if you grew up in Wander."

She'd prayed for an open door in the conversation. God had clearly provided one. "You did." Her hand shook just a little as she opened the baptismal ledger and tried to casually turn the pages as if she were hunting for the right one. "Here."

She could tell the moment when Porterfield's gaze followed her finger to the entry. It was a small reaction, but she was trained to watch for such things. He looked at the entry, then up at her, then at the entry again. "You're Theresa Concord." The words had more than an ordinary weight.

"I go by Tessa Kennedy now, but yes."

There was just a split second where Dawson and Ginny caught each other's eye. "I can see it now. You have your mother's eyes. And her hair. I ought to have seen it sooner."

"Do you remember my baptism?"

"I do. Vividly."

That was a telling choice of words. Tessa took a deep breath and dived into the heart of why she was there. "Does it have something to do with why my father's name is in a different ink? And there's such a long time between my birth and my baptism?"

Ginny pressed her hands together.

Dawson sat back in his chair. "You're not really here about a church history, are you?"

There seemed little point in hiding it now. "Well, it started out that way. I really am researching the town history. But when I found this entry, it struck me as, well, peculiar."

"If you have questions, don't you think they're better asked of your mother and father? They are still around, aren't they?"

Tessa was grateful she didn't feel a wave of I-told-you-sos emanating off Neal. "I figured I'd start with you."

"Have you been talking to Norma Binton about this? She didn't send you up here?"

Neal looked as shocked as Tessa felt to think that Norma was somehow tied up in this mystery. "No. Wait—what does Norma have to do with this?"

"Don't listen to her. She's a bitter old woman who likes to tell stories." The words sounded way too much like a warning. Ginny put her hand on Dawson's shoulder. Tessa got the feeling she was stopping her husband from saying more. More about what?

"Stories? What stories? So there *is* something in how this entry is written, isn't there? Why won't you tell me? What does all this mean?" They knew something. Why wouldn't they tell her after she'd made the trip up here?

"It means you made a long drive for questions better put to your parents," the pastor said.

All the worry she'd been tamping down began to wrap itself around her chest like a steel band. "But I'm here. You know something." She wasn't succeeding in hiding her frustration. "You can't tell me you don't know something. Why won't you tell me whatever it is?"

"Tessa. There isn't anything to tell. And even if there were, you must realize I'm not the person you should be hearing it from."

"But…" There was something. Huge. And now it had something to do with

Norma. She was not going to leave here without answers.

"There isn't anything to tell," Dawson repeated. "There isn't. I'm sure you won't believe me now, but I wish you would."

"But there's something about Norma, isn't there?" Neal spoke up with a sharp tone that startled them all. "Even if you say there's nothing about Tessa's parents, there's something about Norma Binton."

"I think we'd best end this conversation right here," Porterfield said. "Don't go asking me to break confidences as a man of God." He stood, signaling that their visit was over. "Thank you for making the drive up here. I'm not at all sure what it is you came for, but you'll find you're going home without it. I'll be praying you both find peace about whatever it is that's upsetting you."

The pastor wasn't just annoyed; he was upset. As if whatever he was refusing to reveal was upsetting to *him*. There was something going on here, some secret.

Nothing the pastor said would dissuade her of that. How on earth did that man just expect her to get up and walk away after he'd said those things to her? She'd come up here for answers, and instead only received hints that made the whole thing worse.

And not just for her. What about Neal? Was he somehow tied up in all of this? What was God up to, further tangling their lives like this?

Tessa looked at Neal. Surely, he'd choose now to reveal he believed he was Norma's son. If he heard that, Porterfield would surely feel compelled to share whatever it was that he knew. She glared at him, but Neal would not meet her eyes.

And he said nothing.

Tessa wanted to out Neal's secret for him. It felt as if he held the key to all this and was choosing not to use it. Rightly or wrongly, she was frustrated, even angry, that Neal chose to keep his mouth shut with so much at stake. Another part of her knew that wasn't her choice to make. Neal's secret was his to keep or share.

She gathered up the ledgers, reeling under the realization that her past and Neal's were now somehow intertwined. Connected in ways they couldn't figure out. It all felt hugely important and wildly unfair. So many emotions were bumping around in her chest that she barely choked out a farewell to Reverend Porterfield. Neal only managed a curt "'Bye" himself.

Ginny followed them out into the driveway. She hugged herself as if the whole thing had been upsetting to her as well.

"Your parents were special people, Tessa," she said, clearly trying to make amends. "You had a lovely childhood, didn't you? A family of your own by now?" It made Tessa cringe that Ginny looked at Neal when she said that.

It seemed such an odd set of questions for the circumstances. She certainly wasn't going to admit the failure of her marriage to this woman. "Mom and Dad were great," Tessa insisted. "They *are* great to me. I have a boy now, too."

"What more blessing do you need than that?" She took Tessa's hand. "Let it go, dear. Dawson's right. Norma never did know when to let something go. It really is nothing. That's all old wrong pain is, you know. Nothing."

A heavy, divisive silence filled the car as Neal drove Tessa home. They both had so much to say, but each of them seemed to know a single word would unleash a storm of questions and conversations that weren't fit for a sports car careening down a mountain road.

"Porterfield is right," he finally said as they drove past the cheery Welcome to Wander Canyon sign on the edge of town. "You need to ask your parents."

"Well, clearly it's *not* nothing, is it?" she snapped back. "Sounds like it's a whole lot more than nothing, if you ask me."

Neal tried to remember that he'd lived

with the weight of his secret for years, while Tessa just had hers thrust upon her. She was entitled to be stunned. *You could help her. You, of all people, can help her.* He couldn't work out why having Tessa's past involved with Norma's felt invasive. He ought to feel the warmth of a new level of companionship, not the cold defensiveness that currently hardened his spine.

She looked at him as they idled at one of the few stop signs in town. "I don't know what to do about all this. I don't know how we work this out."

You talk to your parents, he wanted to say, but he knew it wasn't as easy as that. If it were that simple, he'd have talked to Norma by now. Splaying someone's dark secret out into the open hurt everyone involved. You couldn't just up and do it like opening a jar. You had to be ready for the consequences.

Neal steered through town toward their block, suddenly aware of how intently Tessa peered out the window. Was she now doing the same thing he always did: Scan every street for Norma? Worry every moment that he'd encounter her and need to figure out what to say?

As they parked, he reached over to help her with the heavy ledgers, but she gathered them up quickly without his help.

"I need to think about what to do next," she said, clutching the books to her chest like a shield. It wasn't hard to see that some part of her had been hoping she would come home from today with assurances instead of more questions. It was a world he knew all too well.

"Me, too," he said.

They ought to talk it out. They needed to talk it out. Only, it seemed beyond them at the moment. Too much weight pressed in the space between them.

Had she realized on the drive home, as he had, that now he absolutely could not leave Wander Canyon without revealing who he was to Norma? It had never really been an option—if he'd been honest—but

Neal felt the weight of that door slamming shut anyway. He had to do it for Tessa as much as he had to do it for himself now.

All the easy comfort of his friendship with Tessa seemed to be slipping between his fingers. "Are you going to be okay?" It felt like such a dumb thing to ask. What he really wanted to know was if *they* were going to be okay. Would they survive whatever piece of the past now connected them?

"I wish I knew. He said it was nothing, but it's not. I don't know what it is, but it's not nothing."

He tried to think of some comforting thing to say as he watched her drag herself up the porch stairs to her back door.

He'd see the light on in her kitchen window early into the morning hours tonight. He wouldn't sleep, either. Too many questions would keep him up. Maybe, just maybe, in a few hours, he'd have his feet underneath him enough to go over and talk to her. That would be the right thing to do. They were better off tackling this thing—whatever it was—together rather than alone. He was starting to need her on some level, and that frightened him.

He was just turning to unlock his own door when Tessa gave an odd cry. He turned to find her staring at a piece of paper. He didn't know whether she pulled it from her mailbox or if it was tucked into the door. The bag of books fell to the porch floor. "Oh, no!" she said, but more in defiance than alarm. "No, no, no, absolutely not. Not before today and certainly not now."

She stormed off the porch back toward him, waving the piece of paper like a battle sword. "I can't believe it. It's like some awful, terrible bad movie. I couldn't make this stuff up."

Whatever it was, it was dire enough to break the awkward silence between them.

She walked right up to him, all the distance of the ride evaporating in her current annoyance at whatever was on the paper. She rattled it in front of his face. "Look at this!"

He took the paper from her. It was a brief note, on plain stationery, in very precise handwriting.

Dear Theresa,
I believe I'd like to adopt one of your kittens. May I come see them Friday afternoon and pick one out?
Sincerely,
Norma Binton

Chapter Fifteen

"She can't have one," Tessa declared.

Neal was afraid to ask why. There were probably a dozen reasons, but it didn't seem like a safe time to ask Tessa to list them.

He opted for the safest reply. "And you don't have to let her have one."

She snatched the note back from him, eyes blazing. "I can't even believe she asked. Norma isn't nice to anyone. Or anything. One of my kittens?" She shook her head. "Oh, no. Not on your life."

Neal would never claim to have what his vet tech called "emotional intelligence," but it didn't take much empathy to see this wasn't really about kittens. He was pretty sure this wasn't even about Norma. This was about how the security of Tessa's family had just been given a very big shake.

Despite all the other complexities of how he'd come to get his family, there had always been one thing he could count on. His parents were authentic, transparent and truthful. They never kept anything from him. The only skeleton in his closet—if you could call it that—was the secret of his biological parents, and even that had been openly discussed and given to him as his issue to address when he chose.

Tessa thought she'd had that security. And now she'd been slammed up against the frightening possibility that she didn't have it. That her parents had kept something from her. That would pull the rug out from under anybody.

What it was, and how big it was, and

even whether it existed at all, no one knew. Except maybe Norma. Wasn't that a kick of the worst kind?

Tessa was pacing the driveway in front of him, still struggling with everything that had happened this morning, still clutching the paper in her hands. "She's got a lot of nerve."

He started with the obvious upside he knew Tessa couldn't see yet. "But," he began carefully, "she's also just handed you a reason to talk to her."

Tessa stilled. That evidently hadn't occurred to her.

"Are you sure you want to just say no?" He went on when she didn't immediately object. He was glad to have the prickly silence between them gone for now. He didn't like feeling distant from her. He'd grown to enjoy—even *need*, although that seemed too risky a word for it—the easy connection between them. He wanted to help her and keep them helping each other. "Maybe the kitten is how you figure out more about her. Maybe as she visits and you talk about the kittens, you can ask her what she knows."

"You're defending Norma? *You?*"

"Well, no. Sort of. As a means to an end, maybe. An opportunity." Was he defending Norma? Tessa wasn't wrong in her reluctance to consider Norma as an adopter. Old Biddy Binton seemed to be the last person in the world who could give love to a little creature like Tessa's precious kittens.

At that moment, his conscience—or maybe Pastor Newton, or even Pastor Porterfield, would say his soul—startled him with the most unlikely thought. *Well, yeah, now. But always?* Right now Norma Binton was a sour old woman behind a drugstore counter. He'd never considered that woman as anything else. After all, she was such a glaring contrast to the mother he'd imagined. Black and white. But what about everything in between?

She had been a preschool teacher. He

didn't know many of those, but the few of his customers who taught young children were the sweetest, kindest, most patient souls he knew. Where was *that* Norma Binton? Did she exist at all?

One more thought startled him even more than the first. What if whatever was involved with the baptism record was part of what had changed her? What if learning what had happened with Tessa's baptism shed light on why Norma was the way she was now? Wouldn't that be important to know as he considered confronting Norma with his identity?

Now you're just imagining things, he told himself. *Seeing connections that aren't there. You want the things to be connected because you want to be connected to Tessa.*

He must have been lost in thought too long, because when his mind snapped back to the present moment, Tessa was staring at him.

"You're right," she said, folding up the

letter and tucking it back in its envelope as if she'd decided the matter. "Letting her see the kittens doesn't mean I have to let her have one, does it? I mean, she *can't* have one. Not yet. They're too young."

It wasn't fair how charming he found Tessa when she was thinking out loud like this. It was an odd—and captivating— thing to be so entertained by watching how her brain connected facts and ideas. Part of what made her a good reporter, he supposed. But it was more than that. He was captivated by who she was as a person. As a woman, a mother, as a daughter, and as the world's most protective kitten rescuer.

"But what will you do if she does pick one?" he questioned. "She might. Right away, like you picked Charlie." After all, every person who had come to see the kittens had selected one to take home once they were old enough to leave their mother. "In my experience, kittens are nearly irresistible. I tell it to people and families all the time. Don't go to the adoption center or pet store to just look. You won't come home empty-handed." While it seemed hard to imagine, Norma might very well be the same.

Tessa's chin jutted out in defiance. "I could refuse. And then what? She'd be grumpy? Ha! She's already grumpy."

She tapped the envelope against her chin for a moment, gears whirring. "But you're right about one thing—this is a way to talk to her without interrogating her. I've done something like it dozens of times for the paper. Kitten fact-finding mission. Who knew that was a thing?"

Neal nodded, the worrisome glow continuing under his ribs. He liked watching her think. He liked her eyes, the way they narrowed and looked off somewhere in search of a solution.

Then those eyes widened and stared at him. Softly, as if she'd just found her way out of the storm of her problem and realized he still had one of his own. "How are you?"

The wave of distance and irritation between them had ebbed. He was entirely too grateful for that. Dangerously grateful, in fact. It showed him he didn't want to untangle the mess of Norma Binton being his mother without Tessa's help. They weren't a couple who'd just had a spat. They weren't a couple, period. He'd best remember that friendship was the most he could offer Tessa right now. "I'm okay."

Was he? He didn't really know.

"I don't get why you didn't ask Pastor Porterfield about Norma being your mother. He knew her around the time you were born. He could have told you something."

"I was so surprised, I wasn't ready to. I figured he'd give me the same answer he gave you, anyway. That the person I should be asking was Norma." After a minute, he added, "He's not wrong. For either of us."

"Either of us," she repeated, telling him that she was as much aware of how connected they'd just become as he was. "I didn't count on our problems tangling up like this."

"Maybe it's not such a bad thing."

The look she got in her eyes told him that wasn't the smartest thing to say. It pulled at him in all the ways he was trying to stop. "Maybe not."

They stood there together in the driveway for a quiet moment, neither one sure of how to navigate this new landscape. "What are you going to do?" he asked just to break the silence.

Tessa pulled in a big breath. "I'm going to say a whole lot of prayers. Then I'm going to invite my parents over to lunch."

He managed a smile. "Good plan."

"But first, I'm going to invite Norma to come look at kittens."

He nodded.

"And you, neighbor, will just happen to be there, providing veterinary advice to her and moral support to me. After all, a conversation about kittens could tell you things about Norma Binton, too."

He ought to tell Tessa that was a bad idea. But he didn't.

Tessa had done a hostile exposé on a reputed gang-affiliated Denver slum landlord. Thirty minutes in a backyard with an old lady and kittens should not make her this anxious. Cute, fluffy kittens should calm the nerves, right? She had Neal there for moral support. If she chose never to veer the conversation off kittens and into possibly dark personal baptismal secrets, no one would know.

Well, Neal would know. But he'd understand. In fact, as they watched the kittens frolic on the blanket inside the pen Friday afternoon, he looked as unsettled as she felt. Norma was now *something* to both of them. Neal knew what that something was likely to him, but Tessa didn't have a clue what it was that Norma was supposed to know about her infancy.

"How'd you sleep?" Tessa asked, just to make conversation. She'd seen Neal's kitchen light on long into the night and knew his night had been no more peaceful than hers had been.

"Okay," he said.

"Liar. I saw your light on," she chided him, needing to know she wasn't alone in how she was freaking out about this. Charlie pounced on her hand and began batting at the beads on her bracelet. The runt of the litter was doing so much better now. She looked forward to the time when he and Dolly would wander the house, sitting on windowsills and basking in pools of sunshine from the living room windows.

"Ah, so you admit you were up to see my light on." He meant to make it a joke, but it just seemed to pull the invisible connection between them tighter. Neal was physically no closer to her than the first day he'd arrived, but he felt closer. He felt nearby, which made no sense and yet seemed to fill a void that had been niggling at her for months. She would catch a look in his eyes, like just now, that spoke of a man's regard for a woman. Of affection. Attraction. Things she'd put on the shelf for longer than she'd let herself realize.

"Hello?" Norma's voice called from behind them, and Tessa felt both of them react.

"Back here, Norma," Tessa called, trying to be cheerful. Talking to Norma now was like trying to balance two different people at the same time—the ordinary Norma and the great-big-secret-not-yet-revealed Norma. Had it always been that way for Neal? Suddenly the dark cloud Neal seemed to drag around with him made sense. The effort to be ordinary with all those questions buzzing around was exhausting.

Tessa had often done her best to ignore

Norma. To steer clear of her. Now, as she waved Norma over to the blanket and pen they'd set out for the visit, Tessa really looked at her. Putting all her reporter's observational skills to use, Tessa took in every detail of the woman. The drably sensible way she dressed. Her bony hands and closely cropped nails. She had pierced ears, but only wore plain small gold hoops that barely qualified as jewelry. No necklace, no bracelet, only a basic antiquated-looking watch. How long was her hair? Tessa had never seen it not trapped in the small bun Norma always wore at the base of her neck.

"Well, there they are." The warmth of the wording seemed so out of place for Norma that Tessa fought the urge to shake her head. Norma settled herself on the blanket, kneeling with her legs tucked so carefully underneath her that Tessa wondered if she should have brought out a chair. After all, Norma Binton didn't really seem a blanket-on-the-grass kind of person. She was more of a straight-backed-chair-at-the-table kind of person.

"Hello, Dr. Rodgers." Norma's formality seemed almost absurd, given the circumstances Tessa knew.

"Hello." Could Norma hear the strained tone in Neal's voice?

"Do they all seem healthy to you?" Norma asked with an analytical tone Tessa would never associate with choosing a pet. A pet was a heart-driven choice. Then again, maybe Norma didn't make heart-driven choices.

"Little Charlie has some issues, but the rest seem fine to me."

Tessa picked up Charlie, suddenly wanting to be very sure Norma understood that Charlie was not available to be adopted. She overrode the petulant "you can't have any of them" tone ringing in the back of her mind.

"And which ones aren't spoken for yet?" Neal was taunting Patsy with a little felt mouse while Tessa let Charlie continue to bat at her bracelet. Almost everyone who came to see the kittens put their hands—and sometimes their whole bodies—inside the pens to play with the kittens, but Norma's hands had not moved from her lap.

"Johnny, Kenny and Patsy," Tessa replied, pointing to each of the kittens in turn.

Norma raised one dark eyebrow in a *care to explain the names?* expression that Tessa was sure echoed the dubious look Neal was so fond of giving.

"Johnny Cash, Kenny Chesney and Patsy Cline. Mom's 'Dolly' for Dolly Parton. All country singers." Norma did not react to her clever naming scheme. "But no one has to keep those names." Tessa stopped herself from saying, "You don't have to," not wanting to further the notion that Norma could actually have one of the kittens.

"I should like a male cat," Norma said, again with a precision Tessa didn't associate with such decisions.

Tessa's journalistic curiosity got the better of her. "Any reason?"

"Simple preference," Norma replied. It didn't sound simple at all. "Company, I suppose."

"Cats are wonderful company," Neal offered. "And they don't require the kind of care a puppy might."

A look Tessa would normally associate with Old Biddy Binton came over Norma's face. "Are you implying I am not capable of caring for a dog?"

Tessa couldn't help but wonder if Norma would dare to ask such a question if she knew who Neal likely was. The woman was an expert at getting under people's skin.

Tessa could almost hear the hair on the back of Neal's neck rise up. Perhaps having him here wasn't the best idea. "A dog is a different lifestyle choice," he replied, a touch coolly. "A larger daily care commitment. Cats can be independent. Left alone for long periods of time. Just seems like that would suit you." The double weight of Neal's words was practically making Tessa's head spin.

"And you know what would suit me, do you?" Norma shot back with a look that again mirrored Neal's entirely too much.

"Can't say that I do." Neal sat back. "But sometimes pets choose the owner as much as the other way around. It's one of the only parts of life that works that way, if you ask me."

This little stunt had been his version of a good idea, but here he was sabotaging it right in front of her. The only thing she was going to learn about Norma in this visit was how much animosity Neal held for the woman. "We don't want to take up any more of your time, Neal. Thanks for stopping by."

Neal glared at her. Tessa glared right back. Her sympathy for his situation didn't quite squelch her annoyance that he was letting it get the better of him. The sharpness of their mutual stare-down seemed to startle even Norma, and she was the stare-down master, in Tessa's book.

Neal eventually got up and huffed back to his door, shutting it loudly behind him.

Norma stared after Neal's sour exit. "What a very unpleasant man."

"He's got issues," Tessa said without thinking.

Tessa called up every ounce of patience she had—and that was considerable, given that she was the mother of a teenager. She tried to adopt a friendly tone. "So, a male cat?"

"Yes." Something softened in her expression. Tessa supposed it was the closest thing Norma had to a smile. She kept waiting for Norma to touch the kittens, to pick one up, or at least put her hand in the pen for them to touch her. Norma simply stared at them. A bit kindly, but also rather analytically, as if she were choosing between brands of cough syrup at the drugstore.

Get her talking, Tessa told herself. "Have you ever owned a cat before?"

Norma's scowl threatened to return. "Is that a requirement?"

"No, but you seem so...specific about your choice. I thought maybe you had some history there. There's a guinea pig now at the preschool, isn't there? Was there a class pet when you were a teacher?" It was a reach, but it would steer the conversation in the direction of those years.

"No, that came later." To Tessa's surprise, Kenny walked over and began pawing at the pen right in front of Norma. As if he was trying to get to her. *Sometimes the pet chooses you.* Tessa was not ready to entertain the notion that Norma could have—should have—one of these kittens.

Tessa dived into her original mission instead. "I was visiting Pastor Porterfield yesterday. He was helping me with his years at Wander Canyon Community Church for a town history I'm trying to write. He told me he hired you as the first preschool teacher."

Norma stiffened—slightly—at the mention of the pastor. "That's true."

"But you weren't there when I went to the preschool."

"I taught before your time there." Norma reached down carefully to put her hand next to Kenny's upturned face. The kitten nudged up against her hand, and Norma made a small unreadable noise at the contact. Happiness? Fear? Surprise? Tessa found it hard to think of Norma having emotions other than disdain and judgment.

"Did you like teaching? I mean, preschoolers are such hard work, I would think you'd have to love it to put up with all the chaos. Greg was a handful and there was only one of him."

"Oh, Gregory was a handful," Norma said without any amusement or understanding. Tessa fought off the image of Norma scrutinizing every student—

especially her son—as preschool board president.

"What do you remember about the church and school during those years?"

She knew the instant she'd pushed too far.

Norma withdrew her hand from the pen and straightened. "What are you getting at?" she demanded with hard eyes.

"Nothing. I just figured you might have a good story for my history."

That had been the wrong thing to say. "Did you?" Norma said icily. "Who told you that? Pastor Porterfield?"

You're in it now. Might as well be in it all the way. "I asked him if he knew why it looks as if my father's name was added later to my baptismal record. Or why I wasn't baptized right away." Norma seemed to be turning to stone right in front of her, but Tessa couldn't—or wouldn't—stop now that she'd started. "I saw it in the ledgers Pastor Newton gave me to look at

for my history research. Pastor Porterfield
told me it was nothing, that I should ask
my parents if I had any worries. And then
he asked me if I'd been talking to you."

Norma began to scramble to her feet
as if she couldn't get out of Tessa's yard
fast enough. "How dare you!" she hissed.
"How dare you invite me over and say
things like that."

"I didn't..."

"What's the matter with people like
you?" Norma went on, her tone pitching
up with anger and something that looked
very much like a long-festering pain.
"Digging up things, poking your nose
into places where it doesn't belong." She
furiously brushed off the grass as if her
clothes were on fire. "Leave me alone.
And you can keep your filthy stray kittens—I don't want anything from you."

Tessa stared after Norma's angry exit.
Ginny Porterfield was wrong. This wasn't
nothing. This was a very big something.

Tessa felt a shock wave go through her as if she'd just stepped on a live wire. Perhaps she had.

Chapter Sixteen

He owed Tessa an apology. He'd been a…
Neal tried to find a kinder word than *jerk*
for the way he'd behaved yesterday as his
feet pounded through a morning run, but
no other word came. Norma's exit from
Tessa's yard had been loud and unfriendly,
and a better man would have gone back
over there and tried to make amends right
away. Only talking—even about cats—
to Norma had brought out everything in
Neal that wasn't a better man.

He'd finally adapted to the altitude and
ran farther and faster than he ever had before, but it wasn't the athlete in him that

drove his pace. He knew better than to try to outrun his problems, but...

Neal's toe caught on an uneven stretch of sidewalk, and he tumbled to the ground, yelping as the concrete scraped his shin. He sat there, panting, berating himself as he watched his knee bleed.

"You okay there?" came a voice from behind him. Neal turned to realize he'd been running past the veterinary clinic and Dr. Davidson had seen him fall. "Rodgers?"

"Caught a toe," he said, trying not to wince as he got up. It had been decades since he'd skinned a knee and he'd forgotten how much what runners jokingly called "road rash" hurt.

"Caught a bit more than that," Davidson said. "Come inside and let's get you cleaned up. Professional courtesy."

Neal followed the veterinarian through his front door and into an exam room. "I ran hurdles in my day," the older man said as he pulled gauze pads and antiseptic from a metal cabinet. "The track jumped up and bit me more times than I care to admit." He chuckled. "Course, other things jump up and bite me now. But then I just charge 'em extra."

Neal had heard some version of a joke like that from every vet he'd ever known. "My tech jokes that pets are free but bites cost double. Her favorite saying is 'I'd rather use a muzzle and keep a friend than lose a finger and a friend.'"

Davidson laughed. "Good one. I'll have to tell Janet." He leaned back against the exam table as Neal cleaned up his wound, handing him tape to hold the gauze pad in place. "I'll miss her jokes, but I won't miss some other parts of this job. I'm tired and I want to spend more time with my grandkids."

"Everybody gets to retire someday." Neal couldn't think of what else to say.

"How much longer you here in town?" Davidson asked.

People kept asking Neal that. He didn't

need reminding of his countdown in Wander. Time felt enough like a lit fuse as it was. The flame was burning down the wire, and it would either end in a bang or get stomped out in a fizzle—he just hadn't decided which yet. "I'm leaving one week from today."

"But you like it here." Davidson didn't phrase it as a question, and Neal could see where this was heading. Again.

"I'm sure you can find someone to take over your practice," Neal insisted. "But it can't...be me."

"And why is that?" the doctor asked. It was a nervy question, considering they didn't know each other well at all.

"I've got a thriving practice in Minneapolis, that's why. I love my work there." He handed Davidson back the supplies. He bent and retied his shoelace, not wanting to meet Davidson's eyes with the falseness of his words stinging as much as his leg currently did.

Davidson was unconvinced. "So much

that you leave it for a month to come and do nothing in a sleepy little town like Wander Canyon? Only, I saw you in church. And at the barbecue. And at the diner."

Just how closely were people watching what he did? "Tessa's been introducing me around." It was classic small-town nosy; nothing that would have happened in Minneapolis. He tried to make it sound like he resented how Tessa was making sure he met Wander Canyon residents, but failed. What Tessa was doing—whether she recognized it or not—was making it harder for him to leave.

"She does that. Everyone does that. For all its faults, Wander knows how to welcome. This place calls to certain people. Sure, most folks grew up here, but others get drawn to it. I was. Not hard to recognize it in someone else."

Neal straightened and set his shoulders in defiance. He was a full foot—if not more—taller than the older man. "Then

I suppose you can count on it calling to the right new vet."

Davidson only smiled. "That's the thing. I'm pretty sure it already has."

Tessa had been watching for Neal most of the morning, looking for some chance to set things right. For someone who'd made a mess of her own visit with Norma, she'd been awfully judgmental of how Neal behaved. And judging other people's behavior was the one thing she disliked most in Norma, so the whole episode had been rather humbling.

I'm not handling this well, Lord, she prayed as she walked into town for her morning breakfast with some friends from the church choir. Usually the choir met on a weekday, but this weekend they'd decided on an extra Saturday morning dose of companionship. That was good, because her friends and scrumptious waffles would go a long way toward making her feel better. *Show me what to do to fix this, will You?*

Pastor Newton would occasionally talk about neon signs from Heaven. Bold, unignorable answers to prayers for guidance that showed up just when you needed them. That was how Tessa would have classified the sight of Neal as she turned the corner onto Main Street. He was in his running clothes, but not running. In fact, he had a sizable bandage on one shin and walked with a limp.

She raced up to him. "What happened?" She was sorry he'd been hurt, but grateful for the easy opening to what still felt like an awkward conversation.

"Took a tumble. I wasn't paying attention and I tripped on the sidewalk. Outside of Dr. Davidson's, actually. He let me come in and patch up."

They looked at each other, then looked away for a moment before they both said "Sorry" at the same time. And then both started an explanation at the same time, talking over each other until they stopped and laughed. Sort of. Things felt tense and fragile between them, and Tessa missed the easy comfort they'd had back before things had gotten so complicated.

"I was a jerk in front of you and Norma. I let her get to me. I'm sorry."

"I shouldn't have gotten so ticked at you. In fact, I did worse than you. She got to me, too." Tessa crossed her hand over her chest. "I blurted the whole thing out, Neal. You should have seen how she stomped off. I didn't learn anything. Except that whatever it is, it isn't nothing."

"What do you mean?"

"She went off like a firecracker when I mentioned Reverend Porterfield and the ledgers. There's something there."

"Wow." Tessa liked that he no longer tried to minimize it. She needed him to agree it wasn't nothing, that it might be a very big something, and she wasn't just on some wild historical goose chase. "What are you going to do now?"

"I think I have to buck up and ask Mom and Dad. But I need to wait until I'm better prepared. I don't want to botch it the way I just did."

A thought—or perhaps another one of Pastor Newton's neon signs—came to her. "Right now, though, I'm going to breakfast with some friends. You should come. It's a far sight better than whatever Pop-Tarts you ate this morning and you look like you should get off that leg. I'll even buy. Consider it my pushy way of apologizing."

She could see him resist. For a man who seemed to want to find his connection to Wander Canyon, he seemed to fight every chance to do so. "I like it much better when we're friends," she added, even though a large part of her was wanting things to go further than that. She'd felt the absence of him surprisingly keenly since he'd huffed off her lawn. She wanted him beside her as she made her way through this murky business with her parents. She wasn't ready to tell other people, and he was already connected to the whole situation even if they didn't know how yet. It felt like she was *supposed to be* connected to him. Not that she'd go so far as to claim it something like Providence or destiny, but it was getting harder to ignore the attraction she felt for Neal.

"I'm not really dressed for it."

"Well, if we were meeting the queen, I'd agree. But trust me, I've shown up in the pajama pants you first met me in and no one cared."

His smile hummed through her, the first warm relief in a span of cold worry. "You looked a lot more adorable in those than I do in these." His face flushed a bit, as if he suddenly realized what he'd said.

Tessa had to disagree. Neal looked rather attractive in his running gear. Lean and fit, with an athletic grace no breathing female would dispute. "I don't know about that," she admitted, willing to meet his small flirtation halfway. "Besides, you'll get the sympathy factor for the injury." Tessa dared herself to hold his gaze. "Come."

"Well…" he hedged. He was trying to resist, and Tessa felt a glow of gratification that she could see he was losing that battle.

"Really. Please."

"Fine. I accept your pushy apology if you'll accept mine. And I can buy my own breakfast."

"Fair enough."

"Brown sugar cinnamon," he said as they started walking in the direction of the dining room at the Wander Inn.

"What?"

"That's what flavor Pop-Tarts I had for breakfast. Brown sugar cinnamon."

Tessa tried to picture it. "My teeth hurt just thinking about it."

His laugh was a welcome sign they'd made their way over this bump in their friendship. This walk felt much more like

the one they'd taken home from the barbecue. *Thank You, Lord. I know this was You.*

"Well, there you are!" Walt Peters said
as they pushed through the doors of the
diner. "And you brought a friend. Hang
on. We'll pull up another chair. Do you
sing?"

Neal looked at her. "Did I mention I was
meeting my friends from church choir?"

"I do not sing. At all. I can barely whis-
tle."

"Oh, well, we'll pull up a chair anyway,"
Walt said. "Mari just made the most wonderful announcement. I was afraid you'd
miss it."

The group all introduced themselves
to Neal as they shifted chairs and place
settings to accommodate one more person at the table. Tessa loved these people
and it felt good to pull Neal into this little circle, even if only for his last week
here. "What?" she asked as she settled
in and poured coffee for herself and Neal

from the carafe at the center of the table. "What's the good word?"

Marilyn Walker's smile could have lit the entire room. "Wyatt and I are expecting."

"Mari!" Tessa jumped back out of her chair to hug her friend. "That's wonderful! Why didn't you tell me when you were over choosing kittens?"

"We hadn't told the girls yet. We wanted to wait until we could tell them they were getting a brother or another sister."

"And?"

Somehow Mari's smile grew even wider. "There'll be another Walker grandson this winter. Wyatt is over the moon. Scared to death, but over the moon."

"He's already a great father to Margie and Maddie. He's got nothing to be scared about," Molly Bradshaw assured Marilyn. Molly had struggled with her own share of parenting challenges, so Tessa knew her words were true. It was heartening to hear all the celebration and encouragement over Mari's new journey into motherhood. Babies were always such a welcome joy.

But were they? As she settled back into her chair, Tessa couldn't help but see Neal's slight struggle at the news. Was he wondering if the news of his own arrival was ever met with such joy? It likely hadn't been. Babies shrouded in secret weren't cause for celebrations by friends. She couldn't imagine Norma even having friends, much less a supportive group like the ones who sat around this table. She wanted to ask him if he was okay, but this wasn't the time or place. Perhaps they'd have a chance to talk about it on the walk home. His time was about to run out in Wander Canyon, and he was going to have to confront Norma soon if he stood any chance of working things out with her before he left.

And he was leaving. Tessa let her heart give in—just a bit—to the sting of that. Looking around the table, she saw friends who had found deep and lasting love in their lives. All of them had lived through heartbreak, and come through to the other side. God had sent Marilyn not only Wyatt to love her, but to add to their family with a baby boy in the coming year. Molly was the canyon's most recent happy ending, finding happiness with Sawyer Bradshaw not only for her, but for her son, Zack. Even beyond this table, Toni Redding had been reunited with her high school sweetheart Bo Carter, and one of the canyon's saddest stories had created a wondrous new family with Jake, Emma and little Cole Sanders. All the women in her circle of friends had left heartache behind to find new love.

Tessa wanted the same. And she was coming to realize that she wanted that happy ending with the man next to her. *I'm falling for him*, she admitted in a tiny corner of her heart. *I'm falling for him and he's leaving. I know I have Greg and all these friends. That should keep me from being lonely, but I am. Greg being gone has shown me just how true that is. When Greg grows up and heads off to his own life, will I still be alone? Just a solitary woman with two cats?*

Tessa tried to shake off her sudden burst of self-pity, but it took effort. And waffles. She laughed and made jokes and tried to make sure Neal connected with everyone around the table. He did come out of his shell a bit, making more conversation than she'd seen him make at the barbecue. He even said—twice—how much he was enjoying his time in Wander Canyon. All in all, it was a lovely time, and she was doubly glad she'd invited him.

Just as they were waiting on their checks, Tessa's phone rang. "Look at that—it's Greg! Early on a Saturday, even!" she boasted, flashing the screen to the group quickly before rising to take the call outside. Nothing could cap off a good meal like the idea that Greg had not only remembered to call, but had called early.

"I'll cover the check," Neal said, returning her smile. "You go talk to Greg and I'll meet you outside."

Molly met Tessa's eyes with an *isn't that nice?* grin. But Tessa waved the knowing look off as she stepped outside to hear Greg's welcome "Hi, Mom."

"Hi there, yourself. It's great to hear from you. Tell me everything that's been going on."

"It's amazing out here. We've done so much stuff. Dad's been great and I've met a ton of friends."

That was practically a gush of information from normally grumpy Greg. "I'm glad you're enjoying yourself. I was hoping you would."

"Yeah, about that. I was…well, I'm thinking… I've been talking to Dad…and I'm wondering how you would feel about me…staying."

Tessa tamped down the cold tendril of panic crawling up her spine. "Like an extra week or two? That might make it tight getting you back and ready for school, but I suppose we could make it work."

She felt the pause on the other end of the call as if it were an avalanche tumbling down the mountain toward her with a destructive force.

"Well, actually, I meant staying. Like, for school and everything. I like the kids here and Dad says the high school here is better than the one at home."

She could just hear Nick's judgmental voice cutting down tiny Wander Canyon's educational system. How dare he even bring this up to Greg without talking to her first? Suddenly all of Nick's super-fun entertainments now felt as if they'd been a campaign to lure Greg away from her.

"Oh," she said, unable to manage more than a single syllable.

"I know we'd have to talk about it more." Greg's tone was unsteady, as if he was well aware of the bomb he'd just dropped.

"You're absolutely right we'd have to talk about it more," she said, probably failing to hide the hurt in her voice. "This is out of the blue, kiddo."

"Yeah, I know. I mean, I'm not sure or anything yet. But I'm thinking about it. I figured you oughta know. We can talk more about it later, right?"

"Of course. Sure. Thanks," she managed to add. *Thanks for the knife right into my heart, son. Thanks for the blindside, Nick.*

She was taking a breath to say, "I love you," when Greg said, "Okay then, I gotta go. Dad's taking me and two guys water-skiing. I'll send you a pic." And he clicked off the call. As if informing her of this drastic choice was just a box to check off before today's installment of nonstop fun.

She told herself not to cry as she sank onto the bench outside the diner.

It didn't work.

Chapter Seventeen

Tessa had been a mess since Greg had called her the other morning. Her subsequent call to Nick had disintegrated into an argument within minutes. She had a dozen logical, important reasons why Greg should come home—why he *ought* to come home. Still, she couldn't seem to bear the weight that none of those sensible arguments held up under the fact that Greg didn't seem to *want* to come home. The rejection stung so hard. As if everything she'd ever done for him, every sacrifice, didn't matter against one amusing summer vacation.

302 Secrets of Their Past

Funk didn't even begin to cover it. Tessa skipped church—something she almost never did. She didn't work, she didn't research or write, she didn't cope with any of the mess about the baptismal records—it all seemed more than she could handle right now. Mari and Molly told her Greg would come to his senses, but that seemed a long shot. She was losing Greg, just like she'd feared. Why had she ever agreed to let him spend that much time in Utah in the first place?

She couldn't bring herself to care what she looked like when a gentle knock on her door came Monday morning.

"Hi," Neal said when she pulled the door open. "I wanted to check in on you. You okay?"

"Do I look okay?"

Neal paused, as if unsure the truth was the safe way to go here. He shifted his weight and stuffed his hands in his pockets. "Um...no?"

"It's okay. I know."

He leaned against the door frame and Tessa found herself so glad to see him it was close to a physical ache. "Got a minute?" he asked.

"Sure," she replied, so glad to welcome him in. "I've got coffee on. No Pop-Tarts, though."

"It's okay. I already had breakfast."

The old Tessa would have found a joke to make about that. Today she couldn't find the energy. This seemed to hurt worse than the divorce, because at least in the divorce she had Greg. Losing Greg left her with nothing. She knew that wasn't entirely true, but the prospect of years alone threatened to swallow her whole right now.

She found two mugs, poured the coffee and slumped down in the kitchen chair opposite Neal. Had she brushed her hair? Had she brushed her teeth? It was such a blessing that he readily ignored the mess she must be.

"I'm sorry." He really was. She could

see it in his eyes, hear it in his voice. The tiny bit of tenderness after all that rejection threatened to undo her and she swallowed back tears.

"There's a big part of me that wants to find Greg and shake him," Neal said with surprising conviction. "How can he not realize? How can Nick not admit Greg is better off here?"

Tessa cradled the warm mug in her hands. "Evidently it's slipping his mind what an amazing mother I've been. Selective teenage amnesia."

"Selective teenage cluelessness," Neal replied. "My mom—well, the woman I know as my mother—was just as amazing. And I'm sorry to say I was probably just as clueless at Greg's age. Maybe even more so. I've had the urge to call her and apologize for all the thoughtless things I've said over the years."

Tessa gave a small laugh at that. "You should. Motherhood is pretty much a thankless job. No appreciation until your kids grow up and wise up—and maybe not even then."

"I hope someday he realizes how much this hurt you."

Oh, that was just the wrong thing to say. It twisted her heart until a tear ran down her cheek, and she pulled in a deep breath and wiped it away with the back of her hand. "If I've done my job even halfway right," she admitted with a wobbly voice, "he'll turn out half as good as you. Tell your mom she did a great job." She ought to have walked back from the compliment, keep from coming so close to telling him how she felt about him, but she was worn too thin for that.

"Actually, that's kind of why I'm here."

"You want me to call your mom?" Tessa was proud she did have a tiny joke in her.

He laughed, and she welcomed the sound. She dearly hoped she'd be in a better place when he finally left and she had to face the prospect of shipping Greg permanently off to Utah without the support of Neal's friendship.

"I'm going to talk to Norma. Today. I thought you should know."

It was good, she supposed, to be reminded that other people had bigger problems in the world. "Wow. Are you ready?"

"Of course not. I don't think I'll ever be ready. But I know I don't want to leave here without telling her, and there isn't a reason to wait. I want to know now. How she'll react, I mean. It could go either way, I figure, but maybe I'll find out something that can help you."

The only blessing in all of this—and it was a tiny one at that—was that this business with Greg put the detail of the baptismal record in perspective. Even if it revealed some horrific fact, it didn't change how much she loved her parents and how much they loved her. She had Mom and Dad, and always would. When Greg looked back over his family decades from now, she had to hope—to pray—that he would feel the same.

"Neal," she said, worrying for him, "I know it feels like your life will change forever after today. Don't give Norma that power." That seemed too much to hinge on the compassion of someone like Norma. Old Biddy Binton wounded people like other people breathed. Disdain was her second nature. "You already have a great mom. Remember that."

He looked down, as if his own emotions were feeling too much to handle. "I know. I called my parents yesterday and told them everything. I asked Mom to pray for me for today. I was…well, I was hoping I could ask the same of you."

The vulnerability of his request cut Tessa to the core, and she reached out to take his hand. It was warm and strong, just as she knew it would be. The way he wrapped his hands around hers felt like the slim foothold she needed. To be needed. That was what she really wanted.

The thing she felt helpless to stop slipping away from her with Greg.

Neal kept his grip on her hand, strong and solid. "I want to try to handle everything well, but to tell you the truth, it feels more than I can handle. I'm afraid we'll just end up hurting each other. More."

More hurt. If there was anything the world didn't need, it was more hurt. "Now?" she asked, suddenly wondering if that was why he was there. "Do you want me to pray now?"

"Unless you need me to make an appointment and come back," he joked. The small smile on his face meant the world to her. *He* meant the world to her—she couldn't ignore that now.

"As it happens, I'm open for walk-ins," she joked back. It felt so good to tighten her grip on his hands to match how he held hers. Here was the connection, the joined hands she'd daydreamed about the night they'd walked back from the barbecue.

Tessa gave Neal's hands a little shake—a "let's get to it" gesture half to knock herself out of the romantic daydream that threatened to invade her thoughts—and closed her eyes. She heard the chair shift as Neal seemed to do the same.

Nick had always claimed to be a man of faith, and while he'd never shown any opposition to the idea, he'd never shown any real passion for it. She'd been very young, madly in love, and too eager to believe how much the love of a good woman could change a man. She'd prayed many times, and he'd said he had, but they'd never prayed together outside of a church service. In fact, despite all the years they were married, Tessa had no memory of ever sharing a prayerful moment as raw and vulnerable as the one now in front of her.

"Lord, loving Holy Father…" she began. "You know our hearts. Our fears, all our faults, the whole tangle of our lives. You know the people we need and the ones who need us. It's all…so…"

She couldn't stop it. The tears were just too strong, the feelings too overpowering, the need and hurt too much to put into words. Tessa sobbed even as she tried not to. It felt like failing Neal, failing herself, failing Norma and Greg and everybody, that she couldn't lay this before God in words. Words were supposed to be her talent. She squinted her eyes tight even as the heat of tears wet her cheeks.

And suddenly Neal was in front of her, pulling her to her feet and pulling her into his arms. If his hands were strong, his arms were even stronger. For the first time in forever, she didn't feel alone. Even if she only got this for a day—for just this moment—it was such a comfort to be held by another lone soul in this world. By a man like Neal.

She and Neal were connected. Deeply. Strongly. In ways they hadn't even un-covered yet.

She'd just have to find a way to live with the fact that it couldn't last.

I should have kissed her. I wanted to.

The thought drummed through Neal's soul the whole rest of the day like a heartbeat. It was almost as loud as his pounding pulse as he turned the corner onto the block where Norma lived. Funny, up until this morning, he would have thought this moment would be the tipping point of his life. Now the moment he didn't kiss Tessa Kennedy felt just as consequential. Was that good or bad? Maybe it just *was*.

Something else struck him so hard, he stopped in the middle of the sidewalk. He didn't want to leave. Yes, part of him wanted some sort of reconciliation with Norma to settle all the lingering questions of his childhood. But another part of him wanted to set things right with Norma for a different reason. If she rejected him, he couldn't see how to return to—or even stay in—Wander Canyon. If he could make peace with her, even establish some kind of relationship with her, there'd be reasons to come back. There'd be a chance to stay. He wanted both those things, not just because of Norma, but because of Tessa.

He wanted Tessa in his life. Suddenly the stakes of the next hour grew sky-high. Tessa had said, "I know it feels like your life will change forever after today. Don't give Norma that power." Only, Norma *did* have that power because she could either ease the way to Tessa or block it. Tessa would never move from Wander Canyon, and he didn't think he could live here with Norma's disdain and bitterness. It wasn't fair that she held that power, but Neal saw no path around it.

Except for God.

Could You do that? Neal found himself pleading as he made his way up the small plain walkway to Norma Binton's windowless front door. No wonder he'd felt such a strong and sudden need for prayer over this—it was bigger than he'd realized even this morning. *Would You do that? Soften Norma's heart so that I can come back? Make a way for me to be part of Wander Canyon and Tessa's life?* It felt like an outrageous, monumental request, a near-impossible feat. But wasn't God in the impossible feat business?

Neal raised his hand to knock, trying to find courage in the prayers he knew were going up to Heaven on his behalf. Mom, Dad and Tessa were praying. He'd even told Pastor Newton that he needed prayers today without saying why. The pastor had, of course, complied without asking a single question. That was the kind of man the pastor was.

He was about to find out what kind of woman Norma Binton was. What kind of mother this woman was, and if she was, in fact, his mother. He knew, somehow, in some sort of bone-deep knowledge he couldn't explain, that she was. Some part of him knew he was her son. It was mostly a matter of what she would do with that knowledge. Or what she wouldn't do. And how his life would change on account of it. The lack of control he felt tightened itself around his chest like rope.

I'm lost here, he prayed as he knocked. *Help me.*

She pulled open the door and glanced at him with suspicious eyes. "Hello, Dr. Rodgers." It was barely a greeting.

"Thank you for seeing me. May I come in?"

Norma led him to a pristine living room, aged and sparse. Straight-backed upholstered chairs with doilies on the arms sat on either side of a small round coffee table. A large, dark bookcase surrounded a fireplace that looked like it hadn't been used in years. There were no photos or mementos on the shelves or the mantel, just books and a loudly ticking clock. Other than the Colorado sunshine streaming through the window, the only bright thing about the room was a pair of still-life paintings on the wall. *This house needs a cat*, he mused.

She settled herself into the chair with the same precision she had on the lawn at Tessa's house. Her arms stayed close to her sides, her hands folded together in her lap, and her legs and feet tightly tucked together. She looked more like the type of schoolmarm to wield a whacking ruler than a warm and encouraging preschool teacher. She looked nothing like the woman he'd imagined his mother to be.

"Are you here to evaluate my qualifications as a cat owner?"

He'd not given a reason when he'd called and asked to meet with her. She probably supposed it was about the kittens. "No," he replied, wishing his voice didn't sound so strained. "I'm here about something else, actually."

"What on earth could that be?"

He'd imagined this conversation for months. He'd rehearsed a dozen different ways to say what he'd come to say. In the end, he could only let the facts stumble out of him in a way he hoped wouldn't shock her. "I believe you and I are related."

Her face lost the little expression she had. "Pardon me?"

It felt as if he was hurling himself down the mountains behind him when he said, "I was adopted in 1985 and I believe you are my mother."

Her hands left her lap to grip the chair arms. An unbearable amount of time passed while she held perfectly, icily, still. "Do you?" she finally said. It was more a challenge than a question.

Neal gave her a quick account of the journey to his assumption, but he got the feeling Norma wasn't really listening. She looked more like a woman scrambling to keep her edges from coming undone. At one point, it looked as if she was actually shaking. Did she find the news of his existence so catastrophic, so unpleasant? He'd expected her to be surprised, but the woman in front of him was mortified. He'd told himself to expect such a response, but the intensity of Norma's reaction pierced him like a blade.

"And that's why I believe I am your son," he finished after his bumbling explanation. It hadn't gone anything like he'd planned. He hadn't counted on repulsion that seemed to come off her in cruel, cold waves.

"What you are," she said slowly, having barely moved since his first statement, "is mistaken."

Neal couldn't say how, but for some reason he was dead sure they both knew she was lying.

So that was it. She would refuse to admit it. Wipe away the facts like a blackboard at the end of a school day. Deny him.

"Are you sure?" His tone was so pleading. So needy. As if the solid, stable man he was crumbled under the weight of her rejection.

His question triggered something in her. "How dare you come in here and make accusations like that? How dare you imply that? Of me? It's disgraceful."

Neal was lost for a reply to her sudden cruelty.

"Have you spread this horrible, vicious accusation to anyone else here? Blackened my name to suit this story you've made up in your head?"

Even though he knew it would only make things worse, he wouldn't lie to her. Not if this was the only conversation they might ever have. "Only Tessa."

Her eyes shot wide at that. "Tessa? You told the town newspaper reporter your wild idea?"

"It's not like that. I..."

She rose from the chair to stand stock-straight and fixed him with the coldest glare he'd ever seen. "I will thank you to leave my home right now. To leave this town. And to never, ever, speak of this to anyone ever again." She made straight for the door and yanked it open. "You're wrong. Wrong. Go away and *do not* come back. Ever."

He had no choice but to leave. Could it really end this way? He tried one last time, extending a hand and saying, "Norma…"

That had been a mistake. "Do *not* use my name," she nearly hissed. "How dare you speak to me that way. Do not speak to me *at all*. I *never* want to hear from you again. Is that clear? Never."

She did not even bother with a goodbye. She simply stood there, gesturing through the open door as if she could shove him out with the point of her jabbing finger.

He walked through the door, feeling as if someone had just chopped off a part of his life. A part he'd never known he'd had, and never knew he wanted. He stopped at the bottom of her stairs and turned to look one last time.

A boldness came over him. After all,

there was nothing left to lose now, was there? "One more thing."

She glared at him that he dared to defy her. She went to shut the door and he walked toward her. She visibly recoiled at his approach. While that hurt, he'd decided something else mattered more. There was only one good thing left to come out of this sorry exchange, and he was going to try for it. "I'll ask my question out here on the sidewalk, but I don't think that's what you want."

She stilled. She didn't invite him back in, but she didn't shut the door. Neal walked back up her steps to stand a foot or so from her. "What do you know about Tessa Kennedy's baptism?"

While Norma did not verbally reply, her entire body stiffened at the question.

"When Tessa went to him to ask about something in the church's baptismal record, Reverend Porterfield asked if she'd been talking to you. You know something." He wasn't going to give her the chance to deny this.

"Why should you care?" The woman had an incredible talent for making words sound sharp and hurtful.

The answer came out of him with astounding ease. "Because I care about her. She's hurt and confused, and deserves the truth. And I think you know what it is."

There was a momentary flash of something in her eyes—pain, perhaps, or regret—but it was quickly iced over with bitter anger. "I know nothing." She said each word with slow, jagged edges. "Now leave."

Neal stepped back. He'd tried. He'd done what he'd come to do, and more besides. The door shut in his face with a finality that seemed to echo through the entire canyon. The sourness, the sheer unhappiness, radiating off Norma Binton stunned him for a moment.

And still, despite everything, he could not shake the absolute certainty this was his mother. His bones knew it. His soul knew it.

"I'm sorry," he said. And he was. More than he could have ever imagined.

Chapter Eighteen

Tessa sat on her back porch swing, huddled under a blanket despite the warmth of the afternoon. *What do I do with all this?* she prayed, at a loss. *Now that I know, what do I do?* She ought to call a friend, or Pastor Newton, to help her sort through what her parents had just told her. Only, she couldn't. It was still too raw, too new. Logically, nothing had changed, and yet it felt like everything had changed.

And she wasn't sure what to do with the fact that the only person she wanted to talk to right now was Neal. Their embrace this morning had woken her up to the fact that she was falling in love with him. She had come to lean on him, treasuring his closeness—emotionally and physically—and that was ending right in front of her eyes. The kittens were leaving soon. Greg wanted to leave. Neal's time here was up in a matter of days.

I'm left. I'm just left alone. She had friends, she had family, but the drowning sense of loneliness threatened to swallow her whole.

She heard Neal's footsteps come down the driveway behind her. The moment he came into view, she knew it had gone poorly. There had never really been very much hope it would go well, but it still sank her lower to see the slump of his shoulders and the hollow, numb sorrow in his eyes. Had Norma denied him? Rejected him? If she truly was his birth mother, either one had to be a profound disappointment.

He said nothing for a moment, just came up and sat next to her on the swing. For a selfish moment, Tessa wondered if his pain would even let him recognize hers. Maybe he didn't need to. They could just be two deeply hurt people sitting together hurting. After all, what words of consolation could come close to doing anything for such large and unchangeable truths?

Truths. Funny how lies and secrets could feel so much better than truths. If the truth was supposed to set you free, she didn't feel it much right now, and neither did Neal. Today the truth had come down on top of both of them like a landslide.

"I'm sorry," she managed to whisper after a long silence. *For both of us.*

He sat very still, looking out toward the mountains in the way she'd seen him do when he'd first arrived. She'd miss his presence, his aloneness that seemed to make hers more bearable. *Lonely together isn't really lonely, is it?*

"She denied it all," he said with heart-breaking detachment. "And I can't even tell you how I knew she was lying. She's my mother, I'm sure of it. And she told me to leave and never come back."

Tessa thought of the conversation she'd just had with her parents, the love and loyalty that still shone through everything they'd told her. Mom and Dad had told her the truth with love. Neal had received lies and rejection. That felt miles beyond fair. Not at all how families ought to work.

"It's done. It didn't turn out the way I wanted, but who am I kidding? There was never any real hope it would turn out differently. Not with her." He pulled in a deep, mournful breath. "So I figured, with nothing left to lose, I might as well ask her what she knew about your baptism." It was then he turned to look at her, his expression changing to alarm when he saw her. His hand went to hers. "Tessa, what's wrong? What's happened?"

The connection she had come to cherish returned, and they weren't alone together—they were *together* together. That made little sense. But what about any of this made sense? "I already know," she said quietly. "I went to my parents while you were talking to Norma. I sort of borrowed your bravery, I guess."

Neal shifted to face her on the swing. "What did you learn?"

"It's complicated." And it was. She wasn't even sure she had the clarity to explain it to Neal, but it would help to try. "It's a long story."

"I'm not going anywhere," Neal said. He meant he was ready to stay and listen, but Tessa's heart heard the truth that he was going somewhere, and too soon.

"There were two brothers. Cattlemen. Pillars of the town family, that sort of thing." It was so hard to find a way to explain the tangled tale Mom and Dad had told her. "Mom had dated the younger one before she got serious with Dad. She and Dad got in a big fight two weeks before the wedding, and this guy tried to move in on her. He got Mom alone one night and…ensured that things got out of hand.

She was ashamed that she'd let him get her alone, that she didn't stand up for herself, afraid no one would believe her word against his. She never pressed charges, never told anyone."

"That's terrible," Neal said. "What a terrible thing to go through."

Tessa remembered the way her mother had cried when she'd recounted the story, and felt her own tears return. "She ran back to Dad, and he never faltered. They realized how much they loved each other and reconciled. They got married just like they'd planned. Of course, they were worried about what might have happened as a result of that night, but Dad decided he'd find a way to raise any child that came into his life from those weeks. His or... otherwise. My dad is the most amazing man."

Concern filled Neal's features as he figured out the implications of what she was telling him. "That's you. You're the child."

"Mom and Dad never told anyone, and

of course, when Mom turned out pregnant, everyone assumed it was a honeymoon baby."

"There were paternity tests at that time, weren't there? Did they confirm things?"

"Dad refused. He said it didn't matter." Tessa's tears doubled as she realized how much more she loved her father today. "He said he didn't want to know, that he'd build the family God gave him, no matter how. Can you imagine? The faith and courage that took?"

"Do *you* want to know?" Neal asked. Of course he'd ask. He'd spent the past month living with the fallout of his biological heritage.

"They *do* know. Somehow—I'm not sure exactly how, but Mom has a theory—Norma knew there was a possibility that the baby wasn't my dad's." Tessa wiped her eyes with a corner of the blanket. "She went to Pastor Porterfield and insisted there be a paternity test before I could be baptized in the church."

"What! Why? She had no right to do that."

Tessa grunted her agreement. "Of course she didn't. But you know Norma. What did Ginny Porterfield say, 'She never did know when to let something go'? Norma threatened to air her suspicions to the whole church, so Mom went behind Dad's back and got the test. She knew Norma would never treat me fairly, knew how hard people could make it for them, and I guess she wanted to know."

"And?"

Tessa sighed. "Turns out I come by my dimples honestly. Dad's my dad. But that explains the blank and the delay in the baptismal records. They never told me because, as far as they were concerned, it didn't matter. Just one dark patch in years of an incredible marriage. And it shouldn't matter. Only, it does, you know? It matters."

The world seemed to set itself a little more back to rights when Neal pulled her into his arms. "Of course it matters." He brushed a lock of hair from her eyes, looking at her with a tenderness that took her breath away. "It absolutely matters. I'm glad you know. I'm sure it's hard, but I'm glad you know." A gentle smile turned up the corners of his mouth. "I learned something important today, too."

"What?" It was hard to breathe with him looking at her like that.

"Norma asked me why I should care about your baptismal record, and I told her it was because I cared about you. And I do." With those words, Neal leaned in and kissed her. A light, careful kiss that spoke of surprise and uncertainty. The kind of kiss that lit up her own heart. When he held her, she could feel the power of the courageous love her parents had known, and still lived. Tessa returned his kiss, and it wasn't careful. It was joy and wonder and a life-giving moment to fight back all of the struggle that might lie ahead. A stunner of a kiss. Given to a treasure of a man.

* * *

"So," Neal said as he pulled Tessa closer, "I guess I did learn something from Norma today after all." It amazed him he could find anything positive, even funny, from the episode with that old woman. But that had far more to do with the woman in front of him, the one who'd somehow made off with his heart when he wasn't looking.

"It's her loss, you know," Tessa said. He took too much delight in her breathless tone. It had been an amazing kiss. He'd known it would be. There was so much life inside Tessa, so much vibrancy. Kissing her was like tasting that joy, pulling it in like a deep breath of the clear mountain air. It seemed silly to feel like one kiss had changed him, but the whole day had changed him—why not a single kiss from such an extraordinary woman?

"She should be busting-her-buttons proud of you," Tessa went on. "Blessed and grateful you turned out to be such an amazing man. She's a hundred kinds of wrong to throw that away." She slipped her arms around his neck, and Neal's heart was no longer his own. He ought to be dizzy, losing so much and gaining so much in a single day. But he wasn't. In fact, he felt more grounded than ever, returned to the footing he'd come here to find.

Neal kissed her again, just because he could and because it felt so flat-out wonderful to do so. He went to kiss her a third time, but she put up her hand to wait.

"Neal, there's more."

"More?"

"Yes. I was going to tell you the rest of it and then I got...distracted." The sparkle in her eyes hummed under his skin. "Very distracted."

He pulled back but kept his arms around her. "Tell me."

"Mom told me Norma didn't come back for the preschool year after the whole thing. She was supposed to, but went away on short notice. The story was she was helping with a sick relative in Colorado Springs, but Mom always suspected Pastor Porterfield sent her packing for the way she'd behaved. Except, she returned the year after that." He saw her gears turning. "What's your birthday?"

"January 10, 1985."

"Eight months after mine." One eyebrow arched up at him. "I just kissed a younger man. Not that it's the real point of this story."

It took him a few seconds to catch up with Tessa's thinking. "Norma went away because...she was pregnant?"

Tessa nodded. "Wouldn't it just be like Norma to try and bring all kinds of fire down on Mom when she'd made a bigger mistake herself? Explains a lot. And to watch Mom get a happy ending while she had to hide in disgrace—well, that could turn someone into as bitter a soul as Norma Binton, couldn't it?"

It made a whole lot of sense. "Porterfield must know the whole story. That's why he insisted on you asking your parents. Since he knew you were really their child, the rest of it wasn't his story to tell. And he'd have no way of knowing who I was and why it might matter."

Tessa gave a huge sigh and settled in next to him. "I started this research looking for amazing Wander Canyon stories. I didn't count on finding one this close to home."

Neal tightened his arm around her. It felt like such a God-given gift to have her beside him like this. He was starting to think he'd brave anything Norma Binton could throw at him to stay close to Tessa. Would God really collide their lives in such an astounding way only to part them at the end of this week? "What do we do with all this?"

She angled her face to look up at him, and if there had been any doubt how hard he'd fallen, it was gone now. "I have no idea." A little bit of sadness darkened the blue of her eyes. "And we don't have a lot of time to figure it out, do we?"

It slipped out of him, illogical as it still was. "I don't want to leave."

She bolted upright, startled. "You...you don't?"

"But I don't know how to stay. I have a full practice back in Minneapolis. And—"

"Dr. Davidson wants you to take over his practice," Tessa cut in, gears turning again. "Couldn't you?"

"What about Norma? She's made it pretty clear she never wants to see me again. Wander Canyon's not that big that it wouldn't get ugly if I ended up staying."

The spark was back in her eyes. "You're not gonna let Old Biddy Binton boss you around, are you?"

Neal smiled at her. "You know, I don't think I will." He *could* defy Norma, couldn't he? The truth didn't have the teeth to hurt anyone but her if it came out—maybe she'd never say anything. If she just kept on being mean to people—

including him—no one would really notice. Sure, it'd be painful to give himself a front-row seat to Norma's disdain, but wasn't Tessa worth it? Wasn't what he'd found here in Wander Canyon worth it?

A new option occurred to him. It only had a tiny chance of working, but it was just the God-sized kind of wonder this story needed to untangle itself.

Tessa noticed the shift in him. "What?" she asked.

"I may have a plan. But it's going to need your cooperation. And I'm not so sure you'll like it."

"If it involves you staying, I'm up for anything."

He surely hoped that was true. "Even giving Norma a kitten?"

Chapter Nineteen

Neal watched Tessa's steps slow as they headed up the sidewalk to Norma's front door the next afternoon. "Do you know how many people I have praying that this works?" she asked.

"Hundreds, I hope." His own palms were sweating. He wasn't especially eager to hear his birth mother lash out at him again. The ice in that woman's stare could frost a mountain range in July.

"Well, not that many. There are only so many people I know well enough to ask for odd prayers, with no hint of specifics. But we have Pastor and Mrs. Porterfield praying, and now that they know everything, I figure that counts for a lot. He told me the whole business was one of the biggest regrets of his time in Wander Canyon."

"My parents are praying. And your parents." Neal still felt a bit uneasy that Mr. and Mrs. Concord knew the whole story. "I don't know what to think of how eager they were to hope Norma really was my mother." There was still a chance he was wrong, but every part of him told him he wasn't. Norma Binton *was* his birth mother. If today failed at letting her acknowledge that, he'd know he'd made every effort at reconciliation. She could choose to cling to the pain of her past, but he was ready to move forward.

"I think they just want to see their daughter happy. And you settled peaceably here. This could be a big step forward in making that happen."

Neal gave Tessa a quick kiss before pressing Norma's doorbell. *Now would be*

a great time for a flood of grace, Lord.
You're probably the only force that could
soften this woman's heart.

The curtains moved in Norma's front
window and Neal caught sight of her
pinched features peering out from inside.
For two whole minutes, the door stayed
shut. Kenny mewed from inside the basket, unaware of his pivotal role in this
story.

Tessa looked up at him. "Should we go?"

Something told Neal to stay. He hoped
it was a nudge from on high and not just
sheer wounded stubbornness. "Not yet."

A minute later, the door slowly opened.
Only a crack, but enough to let Norma
peer out.

Neal was about to launch into the speech
he'd prepared when Tessa stepped forward. "Norma, your son wants to give you
a kitten. Don't you think you should let us
come inside and talk about it?"

If Neal was looking for a sign that maybe
God did indeed still have His hand over

all this mess, it was that Norma pulled her door open and gestured for them to come inside.

They returned to the stuffy little sitting room where Neal had been earlier, only this time the ticking of the clock was accompanied by Kenny's tiny, insistent mews.

"Would you like to hold him?" Neal asked. He wasn't sure where the little ripple of pity for Norma came from. Maybe it was that now he perhaps knew at least part of the reason for her bitterness. Maybe that was what happened when you had lots of faithful people praying for you.

"I suppose maybe I could," she replied.

Tessa lifted Kenny from the basket and tucked him into Norma's open hands. "This is the one who came up to you last time."

"I remember," she said, her voice without its usual edge.

Neal saw a sliver of the transformation he often saw in people around animals.

He'd been surprised not to see any of it in her during that first visit with the kittens. It made her seem extra cold and uncaring to him, and perhaps that wasn't a fair judgment. "Will you tell me the story of what happened?" He realized that he'd never asked before. Just made statements and demanded her response. Let his urgency goad him into confronting her with what had to be the most painful episode of her life. Where were all these new compassionate insights coming from?

"I know about my mom and dad," Tessa added. "What happened to her. Why the record in the ledger is…the way it is. But I don't know how you knew or how the two things are related."

Norma took a few moments to gather her thoughts before replying. "The Taylors were a very well-respected family. One of Wander Canyon's founding families. I expect you know that, if you've been researching."

Kenny settled himself happily on Norma's lap, and she kept her eyes on the kitten as she continued her story. "There were two brothers. Arthur and Victor. Quite far apart in age, actually. Arthur, the younger one, was sweet on your mother before she took up with your father. Handsome boys. Well-liked. Churchgoers."

Neal found it hard to believe Norma was describing the brothers in such glowing tones after one of them had done to Tessa's mother what he did. *People aren't always what they seem on the outside.*

"What most people don't know is that the elder was—" she paused, a faint blush coming over her pale cheeks "—rather taken with me. Or so I thought."

Neal caught Tessa's gaze, her eyes wide with the same surprise he felt.

Norma kept her eyes on the kitten, stroking him softly. "He was still younger than I by a fair number of years, which, of course, made me uncomfortable. A preschool teacher—especially a church preschool teacher—should be above reproach. The day after my mother died, I was terribly upset. Grieving."

Kenny nuzzled his small face into the palm of Norma's hand, and Neal watched the woman's whole body soften in response. He reached for Tessa's hand, not caring whether it would bother Norma to see him do it. His past was about to unfold in front of him and he needed Tessa's touch the same way Norma seemed to need Kenny's.

"My father was not a kind man and I worried about how much he'd want from me with Mama gone. And Vic was so very kind. Full of compliments and promises. I actually thought we would marry. And I…gave in…to a moment's weakness."

She paused, but Neal knew not to speak. She had to tell this at her own pace, wrestling her own pain.

Norma's voice pitched up, became tight. "I was so ashamed of myself. And beyond mortified to discover that none of Vic's promises were true. He had no intention of marriage." Her hand left stroking the kitten to come up against her chest, as if the heartbreak was still fresh. "I loved him, and I told him so. But I was just an amusement to him. A lonely older woman he could pursue for the sport of it."

Her words began to speed up. "When I learned I was pregnant, I was sure my father would disown me. I begged Vic to do the right thing by me, but that's when he told me that if his little brother had no obligations toward Dawn, then he certainly had no obligations toward me."

That's why she pushed for the test of Tessa's parentage. If she could make Arthur pay, she could make Vic. A shock went through Neal as he realized he now knew the name of his father. Victor Taylor.

Norma raised her gaze to Neal, and there were decades of pain in her eyes. "You were a complication to Vic. Something to be smudged out. Nothing worth tying himself to me and nothing that would be allowed to stain the fine Taylor name. A child is not a stain to be smudged out." She spoke the last words with a vengeful conviction.

"So Pastor Porterfield arranged for you to go away. To have me." The last three words felt as if they weighed a thousand pounds.

"You have to remember, it wasn't like it is now. I was ruined. My only consolation was that you would have a better life than you could as a scandal here in Wander Canyon. And Pastor Porterfield struck an agreement with the Taylors that the boys would leave town when I did."

"Well, that's hardly fair," Tessa interjected. Neal was thinking much the same thing. Norma spoke as if she'd given birth to him in the nineteenth century, not 1985. It was difficult. Unfortunate. But hardly grounds to ruin so many lives.

"Oh, I'm sure it doesn't look like justice to you," Norma snapped back, a little of her old self coming through. "But this is a small town. Wander's always watching, as they say. I bear the burden of my mistake every day. In silence. Until you showed up."

He amazed even himself by daring to say, "Maybe it's time to lay it down."

She shook her head as if she found the statement impossible. "You and I both know that's not how the world works."

"You're wrong," Tessa said. "Neal's here. He found you. This whole thing lined up in a way that all this buried truth finally came out. And your son is right. It is time." He heard her pull in a deep breath. "I'm willing to give Kenny a second chance with you when he's ready to leave his mom. How about you do the same and be ready to accept this second chance with Neal?"

Neal's heart sank when Norma offered the kitten back to Tessa. "I don't know."

He rose from his chair. He'd gotten what he'd come for. If this was all the closure he would receive, he'd need to make peace with that. "Well," he said, "when you do decide, you know where to find me. At least until Saturday, when I leave."

They walked back from Norma's mostly in silence. It was sweet the way Neal carried the basket with Kenny inside. She guessed he needed the connection to the kitten now on hold for Norma. His other hand held tight to hers, and Tessa marveled at how good that felt. Walking hand in hand with a man was one of life's most amazing pleasures. *Thank You*, she prayed. *Even if it's only for now, thank You.*

"How are you?" she asked as she opened the mudroom door and returned Kenny to his mother and the litter. The irony of the act struck her. They were returning Kenny to his mother as they'd just, in a way, returned Neal to his.

"Truthfully," Neal replied in a shell-shocked tone of voice, "I don't know. This was an admission, but not really an acceptance. It's better than the denial, but kind of worse. A weird sort of limbo, I suppose."

She touched his elbow. "But now you know. And she knows. It's a place to start. And she didn't tell you to never come back this time."

Neal turned and pulled Tessa into his arms. "She didn't exactly invite me to Sunday supper, either."

"I don't think Norma invites anyone to Sunday supper. Today's the first time I've ever been in her house, and I've lived here my whole life." She nestled into the warmth of his embrace. Even unsettled as he was, he still had a solidness about him, a groundedness she welcomed.

Can You make a way for him to stay? she prayed. *Can You change Norma's heart—or his—enough to let that happen?*

He was still in turmoil, but the dark heaviness that had followed him around those first days had lifted.

"Thank you," he said softly. "For being your wonderfully pushy self today."

"You'll need to get used to it," she dared to reply. "If you stay." She laid her head against his shoulder, delighted to feel his arms tighten around her.

"I want to," he assured her with a tender kiss on her forehead. "I'm just not quite sure how."

"I know I can't ask you to live with Norma's cold shoulder if she can't come around."

Neal tipped her face up to his and ran his hand gently down her cheek. He really did have the gentlest hands. She was just about to fall into a heart-stopping kiss when the house phone rang. She was ready to let it go to voice mail until she spied Greg's cell number on the caller identification. *Don't let it be him telling me he's decided to stay.* Then again, the news might be easier to bear with Neal beside her.

"Don't you answer your cell anymore?"

came Greg's cranky voice the minute she picked up the call. "I've been calling you for half an hour."

She'd put her cell on silent while they were at Norma's and had forgotten to turn it back on. "I was somewhere. What's up? Why are you so upset?" She didn't like the very medical sounds she thought she heard in the background. "And where are you?"

"Dad's a jerk."

Some days I'd agree, but that's not what's important right now. "What's happened?"

"I broke my arm on the stupid trampoline and Dad's like 'What's the big deal? You'll be fine in a few weeks.'"

"You broke your arm?" Any attempts at calm were a total loss. "Are you at the emergency room? Where's your father and why didn't he call me?"

"Hello? Check your cell?" Greg's snarky tone told her he was scared and angry. She didn't blame him. And she could just imagine how Nick's mentality dealt with Greg's first broken bone.

Tessa scrambled to her handbag and yanked out her cell to see three messages and four texts from Greg as well as two texts and a voice mail from Nick.

"Where's your father?" she said as calmly as she could.

"He went to the hospital cafeteria to get us something to eat. We've been here forever." After a pause, and a sniff Tessa suspected was frustrated tears barely held in check, he grunted. "It hurts. A lot."

"I'm sure it does. I'm so sorry, honey. I'm pretty sure it will be okay. You might have to skip a few adventures, but you'll still have a good visit." It was sheer maternal optimism that made her insert the word *visit*.

Greg's voice was low and mournful. "Can I come home?"

The plaintive question went right through Tessa's heart. "Of course you can come home," she said, telling herself not to cry as Neal's hand found hers and squeezed tight. "You might not be able to fly right away, but the minute the doctor clears you, we'll have you booked on a flight."

"Dad's being a jerk." Evidently, Greg believed in repetition for emphasis.

"This kind of stuff isn't his strong suit." Nick could barely handle when baby Greg had an ear infection, much less a teen with a broken arm. "Give the doctor the house phone and my cell number, and I'll wait right here until I talk to him. I'll make sure you get some pain medicines and we ship you home as soon as possible." Tessa felt she deserved a mother's medal for bravery when she asked, "You're sure you don't want to stay? You'll probably feel better in a few days."

"Totally."

Relief washed over her. There was probably more to the reason for his change of mind than a trampoline fall, but now wasn't the time to get into it. "Do you want to stay on the line with me until your dad gets back?" She couldn't believe Nick thought it was okay to leave a barely fifteen-year-old alone in an emergency room. The talk she was going to have with her ex when he called wouldn't be friendly co-parenting. It was going to be 100 percent raging protective mama bear.

"Mo-o-o-m, no." There was the moaning, grumpy teen she remembered. "I'll call you later."

"And so will the doctor," Tessa insisted. "*And* your father."

"Yeah." Greg clicked off the call. Two seconds later, a photo of a splinted arm—with alarmingly black-and-blue swollen fingers—came across her text feed. With the caption Ow ow ow ow ow ow ow.

She showed the image to Neal with something close to a laugh, and then fell relieved into his arms. It was awful that Greg had broken his arm, but it was wonderful that he was coming home.

Chapter Twenty

Friday night, Greg was home in a cast and a sling, and Neal was still trying to work out what the future held. They'd decided to spend what would be Neal's last night in Wander at a local event. Sawyer and Molly Bradshaw were throwing a carousel-ride fundraiser to support a fund for injured police officers.

"I have to say, you look much better than the first time you rode this," Tessa teased as she and Neal and Greg stood in line to enter the event.

"A lot has changed since then." Neal smiled back. Nothing was more true. Even though Norma had not made any overtures since that afternoon, Tessa was standing in faith. Norma and Neal might never truly reconcile, but she still hoped the acknowledgment they had from her could be enough to allow Neal to stay. "Most of it very good." He squeezed her hand as he held it, and Tessa admitted she'd lost her heart.

I love him, she thought. *Should I tell him?*

Neal pulled seven ten-dollar bills from his wallet and pushed them into the silver bucket at the ticket taker's booth.

"That's fourteen rides!" Tessa exclaimed.

"It's a good cause. And I've got a couple of decades to make up for."

Greg groaned. "I hope you guys don't think I'm riding with you. I'm just here to hang out with my friends."

"Really, Greg," Tessa groaned right back. "I could do without the attitude."

Greg rolled his eyes. Tessa kissed him on the cheek just to annoy him. Things had shifted a bit since his return. He was still a grumpy teenager—but there was a little glimmer of appreciation every now and then. His time in Utah had taught him some things after all.

"No rides with us," Neal said. "Duly noted." He and Greg had gotten along surprisingly well. She could so easily envision a future for the three of them.

Tessa smiled. "That was really nice of you. Sawyer was telling me how much a fund like this helped a detective friend of his who had been injured in the line of duty. Can you imagine how hard it would be to recover from something like that?"

"Molly told me the story about Sawyer's friend Dana the other day," Neal replied. "Seems like the least I can do, right?"

Tessa wondered if Neal was on his own path to recovery from wounds. Almost everyone in Wander Canyon was coming to this event. If Norma showed, it would be the first time they'd seen each other since Norma had admitted her story. She didn't know what to expect, and likely neither did Neal.

Cole Sanders came running up to them as they made their way into the big room where the carousel was happily churning through its rounds. "All my turtles are growing great. I got a bigger tank to hold them all, too."

Neal shook Cole's hand. "Congratulations. Seems you've done a great job." Tessa's heart surged at Neal's newfound warmth. It was like watching a new man emerge from the shell of the old one. Every day, his connection with the town seemed to grow beyond what Norma did or didn't do. But would it be enough?

Toni and Bo Carter walked up with brand-new tiny baby Irene—named after Toni's late mother—tucked in a carrier on Bo's chest. "Look at the sweet baby girl!" Tessa cooed.

"It might be a bit early for her first ride, but we couldn't resist," Toni said.

"I figure if she gets dizzy and spits up on me, it'll make a great story," Bo joked.

"That's the spirit," Tessa said. "But if you want someone to hold that precious bundle while the two of you ride, you know where to find me."

Neal tugged on Tessa's hand. "Not until we get at least a few rides in first." Tessa basked in how easily Neal seemed to display the affection growing between them.

They climbed onto the carousel, choosing the two animals they had on their first ride—Neal on the lion and Tessa on the sheep. As they rode through the calliope's cheerful song, Neal reached out and took her hand.

I will tell him, she promised herself. *I won't let him leave without knowing he has my love. But I'd rather not let him leave at all.*

After two more rides, they stepped off the platform to make a stop at the refreshment table. As they chose something,

Molly, Sawyer and Zack came up to thank them for coming.

"How much longer till Blake can come home?" Zack asked right away. "Have you started calling him Smoke yet? Does he like it?"

Tessa laughed and ticked her answers off on her fingers. "He'll be able to go home with you soon. Yes, I call him Smoke now. And yes, I think he likes his new name very much."

"That's all but two, right?" Neal asked.

"Nope. Pastor Newton called yesterday to tell me he'd like to adopt Patsy. And Johnny went to another family from church. So they've all got forever homes now."

"Forever homes are a wonderful thing," Neal said. Tessa dearly hoped he could come to include Wander Canyon in his idea of a forever home.

They chatted with other people, many of whom showed Neal the warm welcome she hoped would help persuade him to stay permanently. Even Greg stepped away from his buddies for a few minutes to say a few words while he demolished a handful of cookies.

After a while, Neal nodded toward the carousel again and said, "Ready for round two? I need to try some new animals."

Tessa marveled at Neal's charm. "Of course."

"You choose first this time," he offered. "And I'll take the mount next to yours."

They were heading toward the bluebird and the goldfish when Dr. Davidson tapped Neal on the arm. "So?"

Neal waved him away. "I haven't told her yet."

Tessa's heart dared to soar. "Told me what?"

"Hop on the bird and I'll tell you."

She grabbed his arm, too excited and hopeful to wait. "Tell me what?"

Neal gave her a look and pointed to the bluebird. She scrambled on as fast as she could. "Tell me what?"

The music started and Neal made a show of pretending he couldn't hear her over the noise.

"Neal Rodgers, don't make me come down off this bird…"

He laughed and then reached for her hand again. "I'm taking over Dr. Davidson's practice. I'm staying in Wander Canyon," he shouted over the music.

"No matter what N—" Tessa realized it wasn't her place to shout the name "—*she* says?"

The warmth in Neal's eyes outshone any of the carousel's twinkling lights. "No matter what *she* says. I'm staying."

The animals may have been spinning around, but she was dizzy with happiness. It wasn't at all how she'd imagined it, but nothing could have stopped her from silently mouthing the words *I love you* to him as the music swirled around him.

He heard her message loud and clear. Neal squeezed her hand and silently said *I love you, too* right back. There wasn't a louder sound in the universe than the silent declarations they'd just made. Tessa would have given anything to climb down off that bluebird and kiss that man senseless in front of everyone.

She was getting ready to do just that as the carousel slowed, but stopped herself when she saw Neal's face change. She turned toward the entrance to see Norma Binton come tentatively through the doors. The old woman scanned the room, her eyes widening when she met Neal's gaze. Her face changed into a look of fragile vulnerability Tessa had never seen.

Neal looked at Tessa, a hundred emotions playing across his own face. She released his hand and nodded. "Go."

There were still all kinds of noises and lights in the room, but all of it seemed to fade as Tessa watched Neal walk over to Norma. The world held still as they regarded each other for a moment.

"Would you like to ride the carousel?"

he said. His voice was thick with the emotion of the moment. He held out his hand.

Tessa felt tears well up in her eyes as Norma hesitated, then placed her small hand in Neal's. "I believe I would."

Tessa lost her battle to the tears as she watched Neal gently lead Norma up to the one bench on the carousel, sitting beside her. Every tangle in the world seemed to set itself to rights as the platform began to move and mother and son took a carousel ride decades overdue.

A handkerchief appeared in her vision and Tessa turned to see Pastor Newton. "I should ask you what just happened over there, but I think I already know."

"Yes," she said with a glow she knew wouldn't leave her soul for a very long time, "I expect you do, too."

"This just might be my favorite happy ending of all," the reverend said.

Tessa could only smile through her tears. "Mine, too."

* * * * *

Dear Reader,

There was really only one way to say goodbye to Wander Canyon. When the idea to redeem Old Biddy Binton came to me, I knew it was the perfect story to end what has been a beloved series. And certainly Tessa, who had been such a faithful friend to many, needed her own happy ending.

So many of us struggle with pasts that weigh us down. We forget how God delights in forging abundant futures for us, if we will only trust Him to do so. No cause is ever really lost with God.

I mention Sawyer's friend, wounded police detective Dana Preston, in that last scene for a reason. My next series, Camp True North Springs, features Dana, who has an adventure of love and faith awaiting her…as do you, dear reader.

I'd love to hear how this series has touched you. Find me on Instagram, Facebook, Twitter, and at alliepleiter.com, or by mail at PO Box 7026, Villa Park, IL 60181.

Blessings,
Allie